"I don't like seeing you so angry at everything, Simon."

"Why?" He held his breath, braced for Joy's answer.

"Because I care about you. We're friends, at least I hope so."

Her statement sent a warm flow around Simon's heart. "We are." He resisted the urge to brush a stray strand of hair from her forehead. "You're a very optimistic person."

She smiled. "I'm also known for being obstinate."

"I like you obstinate. I like you cheerful. I didn't realize what I was missing until you came along."

She looked into his eyes and the air between them sparked like the lightning outside the window. Joy held his gaze a moment, then stepped back.

"Good night, Simon."

She walked away, leaving him with a cool chill on his skin and an uncomfortable knot in his chest. His feelings for Joy were growing and he had to find a way to stop them...

Lorraine Beatty was raised in Columbus, Ohio, but now calls Mississippi home. She and her husband, Joe, have two sons and five grandchildren. Lorraine started writing in junior high and is a member of RWA and ACFW, and is a charter member and past president of Magnolia State Romance Writers. In her spare time she likes to work in her garden, travel and spend time with her family.

Books by Lorraine Beatty

Love Inspired

The Orphans' Blessing
Her Secret Hope
The Family He Needs

Mississippi Hearts

Her Fresh Start Family
Their Family Legacy
Their Family Blessing

Home to Dover

Protecting the Widow's Heart
His Small-Town Family
Bachelor to the Rescue
Her Christmas Hero
The Nanny's Secret Child
A Mom for Christmas
The Lawman's Secret Son
Her Handyman Hero

Visit the Author Profile page
at Harlequin.com for more titles.

The Family
He Needs

Lorraine Beatty

LOVE INSPIRED
INSPIRATIONAL ROMANCE

LOVE INSPIRED®
INSPIRATIONAL ROMANCE

Recycling programs
for this product may
not exist in your area.

ISBN-13: 978-1-335-75884-2

The Family He Needs

Copyright © 2021 by Lorraine Beatty

This edition published by arrangement with Harlequin Books S.A.

For questions and comments about the quality of this book, please contact us
at CustomerService@Harlequin.com.

Love Inspired
22 Adelaide St. West, 40th Floor
Toronto, Ontario M5H 4E3, Canada
www.Harlequin.com

Printed in U.S.A.

This is the day which the Lord hath made;
we will rejoice and be glad in it.
—*Psalm* 118:24

To my precious mother-in-law, Mary Beatty,
one of my biggest blessings.

Chapter One

Joy Duncan checked her appearance in the bathroom mirror one more time, then sent up a quick prayer for strength. She started her new job today, thanks to Ray Graham, a regular customer from the diner where she had worked in the small town of Blessing, Mississippi. Fire had damaged the eatery and the apartment above, where she and her five-year-old son, Mikey, had lived. After finding herself homeless and unemployed, she and Mikey were now sharing a one-bedroom studio with her cousin Willa Carter, who owned the diner.

Joy's faith had been shaken after the fire. There weren't many jobs in Blessing that would support a single mom. However, the Lord had come through for them again. Ray had called last night informing her he'd arranged a job for her as the assistant to local newcomer Simon Baker. All she had to do was report for work.

Walking into the small living area, Joy smiled at her son, who was playing with little cars on the floor with Willa. Though there was twenty years between them, she and her cousin had always been close. She had offered the job and the apartment two years ago after Joy's husband, Chad, abandoned them.

Willa glanced up and smiled. "You look fantastic."

Joy smoothed the front of her navy slacks and touched the collar of her pale green blouse. "It does feel good to be out of that waitress uniform." Mikey looked up and smiled, melting Joy's heart into a warm puddle. "Are you and Willa playing cars?"

"Uh-huh. We had a big crash and the cars went ga-doosh." He demonstrated with his hands flailing outward.

Willa stood and came to her side. "Are you sure working for Simon Baker is a good idea?"

"Of course. Why not? The salary is generous and the job comes with an apartment."

"I know, but you've heard the talk. He was a real hellion when he lived here as a kid. He had a chip on his shoulder a mile wide, always angry and spoiling for a fight and running headlong into serious trouble."

"That was a long time ago. He's a grown man now."

"Maybe, but why is he hiding? He's been in town for three months and I never see him at the diner or at church or anyplace else, for that matter."

Joy had no answer for that. Baker had kept a low profile since returning to Blessing and rumors about him had been flying like dandelion puffs in the wind. It wasn't every day that the town's former bad boy inherited the prestigious Afton Grove estate. "Maybe he's busy managing his new wealth, or maybe it's because of that scar we've heard about."

Willa nodded. "Every time I hear it mentioned, it gets bigger and uglier. You'd think he was giving Frankenstein's monster a run for his money. Though, no one that I know has actually seen the man, except for Ray."

Joy took the small car Mikey handed her. "I don't care what he looks like. I'm just grateful for the work."

Willa huffed. "I want to know what he's going to do about the bridge now that he owns the land."

Joy wanted an answer to that question, too. The Blessing Bridge was the very heart of the town. Previous owners of the estate since the 1950s had granted public access to the landmark, which stood in the old gardens of Afton Grove. With Blessing's bicentennial coming up next year, the city council wanted to beautify the garden surrounding the bridge. The lease agreement was up in six weeks and the town was growing anxious. They needed to know Baker's intentions. Their greatest fear was that Baker would sell the land and they'd lose the bridge forever.

Picking up her purse, she patted Willa's arm. "Maybe I can find out his plans since I'll be working for him."

"I hope so." Willa gave her a hug. "Promise me one thing. If you don't feel comfortable with Baker, you'll quit. The rumors about him make me nervous. What if he's dangerous?"

Joy laughed. "That's ridiculous. The rumors are only wild because no one knows anything about him other than he's the kid from the wrong side of the tracks who inherited the town's historic estate." Joy ignored the flicker of concern that pricked her nerves. "I need this job, Willa. Whatever the circumstances, I'll manage."

Despite her brave front to her cousin, Joy's anxiety churned as she drove the short distance to Afton Grove. This was not the job she would have wished for, but she couldn't turn her back on a gift. Pulling her old car to a stop in front of the impressive Queen Anne Victorian, she took a moment to appreciate its stately turrets and gingerbread. A wide porch wrapped across the front and around one side. If nothing else, she'd enjoy working in this incredible house. Unfortunately, the house was also weathered and dilapidated. It was the kind of place Stephen King would write about. A grizzled old recluse with a scarred face burying himself in the bowels of a creepy old house, waiting to capture anyone who knocked on the door.

Joy shook her head to dislodge the ridiculous thoughts. Taking a deep breath, she approached the door, trying not to think about all the negative comments she'd heard about Baker. She pushed the bell beside the massive front door with shaky fingers.

The door opened and a tall, dark-haired man glared at her. She swallowed the sudden lump in her throat. Maybe she should have listened to Willa. Baker was more intimidating than she'd anticipated. His broad shoulders dominated the doorway and his intense gaze caused a sudden skip in her heartbeat. Her attention landed on his scar. It started at his temple and trailed down across his high cheekbone to the side of his mouth. The rumors she'd heard had been exaggerated. His scar was hardly the thing nightmares were made of. It wasn't his scar that had her concerned, it was the scowl on his face and his attitude.

"Yes. What do you want?"

His deep voice sent a tremor along her nerves. "I, uh…" She cleared her throat. "Mr. Baker, I'm Mrs. Duncan. Ray Graham told me to report to work today."

The man's scowl deepened. "I was expecting a Jay Duncan."

"No. Joy. Joy Duncan." She held her breath, her heart aching. This was all a big mistake. There was no job and no apartment. Someone had messed up.

The man rubbed his forehead. "You'd better come in." He waited for her to enter then shut the door and walked ahead. "Ray's message said Jay."

"Corrective text strikes again." Her feeble attempt at humor fell flat. She followed him into a large room she guessed had been the parlor. An office area had been set up in the center. He gestured for her to be seated. Gauging from the irritated expression on his face, she would be job hunting again tomorrow.

He stood behind his desk, staring at something on the surface. The morning sunlight from the large window silhouetted Baker's height and trim physique. He was much younger than she'd expected. From the chatter floating around town, she'd envisioned a man in his fifties. This man was closer to midthirties.

He looked up suddenly and her heart skipped a beat. The scowl on his chiseled features drew his dark brows together and pulled the corners of his generous mouth downward into an angry frown. The dark jeans he wore and the oxblood shirt did nothing to soften his appearance.

"Do you know your way around a computer?"

"Yes." She clasped her hands together tightly in her lap. "I've worked as a secretary for many years."

"Any real estate experience?"

"No, but I'm sure I can pick it up quickly."

His penetrating gaze suggested he was skeptical.

"How do I know you won't find a more interesting job and quit?"

Joy gritted her teeth at the insulting question but looked him in the eyes. "Because I need this job and I have a son to support. And I don't walk away from my responsibilities."

She started to smile to emphasize her point but it died on her lips. His expression was so dark and foreboding, it was like trying to smile into a black hole. But then she looked into his eyes and her heart shifted. The brown depths were filled with pain. A pain she recognized. He'd lost something or someone and he'd never recovered. She started to offer a word of comfort but quickly changed her mind. This was not a man who would welcome any intrusion into his private world. Ever.

Simon held her gaze. "Are you prepared to start today? I can't afford to get any further behind."

"Yes. Of course." Inwardly, she released a deep sigh of relief.

"Good." He sat down, all business now. "I'll need you to help manage the estate and the properties attached to it. Apparently, even run-down buildings and old houses need constant attention. Hopefully, it'll all be gone soon."

Joy's spirits sagged. "So this isn't a long-term position?"

He glanced at her with his shadowed eyes. "Only until I can unload everything. The sooner the better."

"Oh." Joy's mind whirled. It had never occurred to her Simon would want to sell all of his inheritance. "You're planning on selling the estate?" What about the bridge? Was he going to sell it, too? She held her breath.

He stood. "Your office is over here in the alcove."

She followed him into the small adjacent space, which held a desk with a computer, a few storage cabinets and a cozy chair beside a floor lamp. The soft green color and the faded wallpaper filled her with a sense of calm. Something she might need if she was working for the ill-tempered Simon.

Joy quickly refocused. First things first. "I was told a furnished apartment came with this position." He hesitated a moment before responding, as if reluctant to acknowledge that benefit.

"Yes. The former servants' quarters were converted into an apartment."

"Would it be possible to see it now? I'm anxious to get my son settled as soon as possible." From the stony expression on his face, she thought he might refuse.

"Of course." He retrieved the key from the desk drawer then led her from the office.

She had to hurry to keep up with his longer stride and still take in the splendor of the old home. The intricately carved wood trim, stained-glass window on the stair landing and dark wood floors were all stunning. Unfortunately, the home's interior was as badly neglected as its exterior. The furniture and carpets were threadbare and the wallpaper was peeling in spots. "You have a wonderful home."

"It's not my home. I just own it." He unlocked a door at the end of the back hall, waiting for her to enter.

She stepped inside and smiled. "Oh, how lovely. I had no idea it would be this large." The living room was cozy and inviting, with a fireplace and large mullioned windows. "It'll be nice to have some space again." She peeked into the two bedrooms then strolled into the kitchen and laid her hand on the stone countertop. "Perfect for making cookies."

"Cookies?"

"Mikey and I like to bake." She looked out the window. "Oh, what a big yard. Mikey won't have to be cooped up in an apartment anymore. He can run and play and, oh, maybe I could hang a swing from that tree limb."

She turned to smile at Simon but he was scowling again, making her remember that she still had a full day of work ahead. "Thank you. You have no idea how much this means to me and my little boy. When can I move in?"

"Whenever you want." He handed her the key and walked off.

Working for Simon Baker might be difficult, but it was a small price to pay for a home of their own again and freedom from financial worries. This job paid twice what she'd been making at the diner. Taking a deep breath, she gathered her determination and headed back to the office for her first day of work for the ever-scowling Simon Baker.

Simon made his way to his own kitchen on the other side of the house, his irritation swelling with each step. *Thank you. You have no idea how much this means to me and my little boy.* The words had pierced his emotional armor, sending his defenses slamming into place. He should never have offered the apartment with the job. It had worked well when his former assistant, John Moore, was living there. It would be a different situation now. Having a woman and child underfoot all day would be more than he could tolerate. The old Victorian house was large but not that large. Pulling out his cell phone, he then punched Ray's number, not waiting for him to speak. "What are you trying to do?"

"About what?"

Simon gritted his teeth. "Mrs. Duncan. I thought you were sending a man."

Ray chuckled. "Nope. I sent an attractive young woman instead. You complaining?"

Simon bit his tongue to keep from swearing. "She's totally unsuited for the job. I don't appreciate your little joke."

"It wasn't a joke, pal. She's perfect. She's smart as a whip and a hard worker."

"She has a child." Simon rubbed his forehead and paced the kitchen. "She'll be asking for time off for her sick kid and running off to school events or the doctor."

"She lost her job and her home because of that fire in the Hanson building last month."

Simon exhaled an irritated breath. "She was a waitress? And you want her to be my assistant? I guess she can bring me coffee and lunch."

"Stop being a jerk, Simon. Joy's a single mom trying to raise her son on her own. Show a little compassion."

Simon clenched his fist. He was low on that attribute right now. Sorting through his uncle Oscar's records was frustrating and tedious. If he was a real businessman, he might understand the details better, but he was a pilot, trapped in a real estate mess that he had no power to clean up. "I just need someone to step in and handle the paperwork and keep the details straight.

I've got to get these properties sold in the next couple months before all the taxes come due. I've already been in this town too long."

"Then, if you want an assistant to speed things up, Joy's your only option. Child and all. There's no one else in town available at the moment. The sooner you get these buildings sold, the sooner you can go home."

Home. He didn't have a home. Hadn't since Holly and the baby died. Simon ran a hand down the back of his neck. He resented being forced into a corner. There was no way he could work with that woman daily let alone have a child running around the house. It would be like pulling a scab off a barely healed wound.

"Simon, I understand what you're dealing with being back here in Blessing, and I know having Joy and her son in the house will be uncomfortable, but at some point you've got to forgive what happened. That goes for the accident, as well."

Simon's throat tightened. Why did no one understand? "I'll never forgive this town for what they did to my mother and I'll never forgive that boy who took my family from me."

"It was an accident, Simon. No one's fault other than ice-covered streets and human error."

"No. I heard the police officer say it was a drunken boy and I'll never forgive him."

"I hope you will someday." Ray rubbed his forehead. "Simon, this isn't who you are. I know losing Holly and the baby was hard, but you've got to move on."

Hard? Running a marathon was hard. Scaling a mountain was hard. Losing his wife and unborn child was unbearable. Simon squared his shoulders. "I have work to do."

"Give Joy a chance. You won't be disappointed. In the meantime, I'll keep an eye out for someone else."

It wasn't like his friend to push him into anything. "Why do you care so much?"

"Because she's a nice lady and she's been through some tough times, but she always had a smile and a kind word for me at the diner no matter how difficult things were."

Simon's resistance waned a bit. He and Ray had been friends growing up, and when Simon returned to Blessing three months ago, they'd picked up where they'd left off. An attorney, Ray had been a huge help dealing with the inheritance.

Simon quickly weighed the pros and cons. He had three downtown properties and the Afton Grove estate to sell, and so far not an offer on any of them. He needed every penny from this inheritance if he was going to go back home to Charlotte to start his air charter service. Airplanes didn't come cheap. Besides, his investor wasn't going to wait forever and without him there wouldn't be a charter service at all. He rubbed his forehead. Having someone to help was better than having no one at all. He could afford to try her out for a few weeks. "Fine."

"Joy's a keeper. You won't regret it."

"I already do." He regretted his return to Blessing, too. The town never cared about him or his family when he was growing up here. As distant relatives of the esteemed Templeton family, who had owned Afton Grove since before the Civil War, the Bakers were considered black sheep and not worth consideration.

"Good. Just give her a chance, Simon. The little boy, too. They might end up being a blessing."

Simon ended the call. Nothing in this town could be called a blessing. To him, happiness was Blessing in the rearview mirror and as soon as possible. But he had to accept the inevitable. If he was going to stay on top of things, he had to work with this woman.

His new assistant was seated in front of his desk when he returned to the office. She glanced up and smiled. He tried to sound pleasant but he knew he failed miserably. "John, my former assistant, has all the files you'll need on his computer. Why don't you take this morning to look those over then take the rest of the day off. We'll go over your responsibilities tomorrow."

She smiled. "That'll be fine. Thank you." She rose and went into the alcove.

Simon wished she had a separate, enclosed space to work. Having John close at hand had worked well, but Mrs. Duncan so close could be a distraction. He breathed a sigh of relief when she left around one o'clock.

Ray was right. She was attractive. Her smile was bright enough to light up a room. In fact, he'd fought the urge to pull down the blinds to shade himself from it. There was a sparkle in her bright blue eyes and a shimmer to her auburn hair. The word *vibrant* came to mind. But he wasn't looking for a pretty assistant. He needed a competent one and that was yet to be determined.

Still uneasy with his new hire by late afternoon, Simon decided a good run would work off some irritation before supper. One nice thing about inheriting the estate was the endless options for running. He could go for miles and never see a soul. Just the way he liked it.

An hour later he entered the back door and started down the hall. The apartment door suddenly opened and a small person burst like a rocket into the hall, stopping in front of him. The boy had to be Mrs. Duncan's son. He was a carbon copy of his mother. Bright blue eyes filled with curiosity and a smile that lit his whole face.

"Are you a giant like in 'Jack and the Beanstalk'?"

The question caught Simon off guard. He wasn't that tall, a tick over six feet, but to a little boy he might look like a giant. He cleared his throat. "No. I'm not."

"Are you the king?"

"What?"

"This is a castle, isn't it? What's your name?"

Simon searched for a way to remove himself from this uncomfortable situation. "It's Simon."

The boy smiled and held up his hand, fingers spread wide. "I'm Mikey. I'm five."

Was he supposed to reveal his age, as well? Before he could respond, the boy moved closer, his expression puzzled.

"Does your boo-boo hurt?"

Simon resisted the impulse to cover his scar with his palm. He raised his eyebrows. "No."

"Mine doesn't hurt, either." He shrugged. "Well, sometimes."

He held up his hand, sending ice through Simon's veins. The boy's left hand was deformed. The two middle fingers were missing, leaving only the thumb and forefinger and pinkie. Speechless, Simon could only stare and ache for the child's handicap.

"Mikey, come back here." Joy appeared out of the apartment door and hurried toward her son, placing her hands on his shoulders protectively and keeping him close to her body. "I told you this isn't part of our house. Wait for me in the kitchen."

"Yes, ma'am." He turned and waved. "Bye, Simon." He disappeared as quickly as he'd come.

Simon looked at the mother, his mind spinning with questions. "His hand. It's... I didn't know he was..."

Joy's blue eyes turned a stormy gray. "Handicapped. Deformed? A freak?" She crossed her arms over her chest. "My son isn't handicapped or challenged or any of those ugly words. He's perfect. He can do anything any other child can do. He's happy and healthy and loving. Nothing else matters."

Simon's cheeks flamed. "No, I didn't mean... I'm just..."

She squared her shoulders then turned and marched off, leaving Simon with a sick sense of shame in his chest. He might have just lost his only candidate for an assistant. Mrs. Duncan would probably quit and he couldn't blame her.

Joy reported to her office early the next morning, hoping to be deep into her work when Simon arrived. She'd spent a sleepless night riddled with regret at her attack on him yesterday. She tended to be overprotective of Mikey, especially when it came to his hand. Any hint of shock or disgust would set her off. Too late she'd realized that she hadn't told Simon they would be moving in that afternoon, so he'd been caught off guard and then blindsided by Mikey. She should have taken that into consideration and explained things.

Her first goal this morning was to clear up the misunderstanding. If he'd let her. She braced at the sound of footsteps shuffling on the carpet. He stepped into her alcove and stopped at her desk. She put on a smile she didn't feel. "Good morning."

He frowned. "I hope you settled into the apartment all right."

"Yes. And I'm sorry I didn't tell you we were moving in yesterday. Since I got off work early, I thought we might as well take advantage of the time."

Simon's brow furrowed. "You moved everything in that quickly? I was only gone from the house for an hour or so."

"There wasn't much to move. The fire trimmed our belongings down to the bare bones." She took a deep breath. "I want to—"

"I need to—"

They'd spoken at the same time. Simon waited for her to speak. "I shouldn't have attacked you about Mikey. I'm so sorry."

Simon shook his head. "No. I'm the one who should apologize. I gave you the wrong impression. I was surprised, that's all. It seemed unfair for such a little guy."

"I learned a long time ago life isn't fair."

Simon met her gaze. She could sense he was searching for words.

"May I ask about your son's hand?"

His tone was sincere, so she decided to explain. Most people had questions when they first met Mikey. Being up-front about it had proven to be the best policy when dealing with people's curiosity. "Amniotic Band Syndrome. It happened when I was carrying him. The tissue wrapped around his arm. I had surgery to try and correct it and they cleared it off except for his hand. We were very blessed."

Simon scowled. "Blessed?"

"Of course. It could have been much worse. He was in danger of losing his hand." Joy could see he was conflicted. She understood only too well. It might have seemed unfair for a little boy to be born with fingers missing on one hand, but it had never slowed Mikey down. Ever. And that was something to celebrate. "Mikey is a perfectly normal, happy kid. We don't need to be angry for him or feel sorry for him. Everyone has some kind of cross to bear. Either physical or emotional." Simon's hand went to his cheek. She spoke without thinking. "How did it happen?"

He didn't pretend to not know what she meant. "A car accident."

"I'm sorry. But it's not as bad as I expected. It could have been worse, I suppose." Simon's brown eyes turned black. The muscle in his jaw flexed rapidly.

"It was. I lost my wife and unborn child." He pivoted and walked out.

Joy wanted to bite off her tongue. Why couldn't she leave well enough alone? Now she understood the pain she'd seen in his eyes. Maybe she should apologize. Or maybe she should let things calm down. Either way it was going to be a long day.

It was late afternoon when Simon called her into his office. Joy had come to terms with her faux pas. Simon had acted as if nothing had happened as he'd gone over her responsibilities and she'd done likewise. Picking up the few bills she needed to ask about, she went into his office, handed them to him then sat down. "I had no idea there was so much to managing empty buildings. Do you have offers on them?"

"No. Apparently no one wants real estate in a small town."

Joy had to ask. It was crucial to everyone in Blessing. "What about the bridge land?"

"What about it?"

"Surely you're not going to sell it, too?"

"Why not? It's of no use to me."

She couldn't believe what she was hearing. "But it's important to the town. It's been the symbol of our community for decades. Why are you so anxious to sell everything?"

"Because I have plans to start my own business and I can't do that until I rid myself of this inheritance."

Joy's heart sank. How could Simon be so oblivious to the importance of the Blessing Bridge? His attitude increased her concern, making it hard to focus as he went over the list of things he wanted done. Back in her alcove, she tried to concentrate on her work but worry over the future of the bridge made it difficult.

Picking up the stack of mail on her desk, she sorted through the envelopes. One letter caught her attention. Most of Simon's mail was addressed to Simon Baker. This one was Simon J. Baker. Something about the name stirred a vague recollection but she couldn't pull it up.

The elusive feeling was still teasing her later that afternoon, yet each time she reached for the memory, it would dissolve like mist then turn into a migraine. A severe concussion several years ago had left her with headaches and gaps in her memory They were usually triggered by stress and working for Simon was stressful.

She shrugged off the odd impression as nothing more than Baker being a common name.

What else could it be?

Chapter Two

Simon glanced up as Ray entered his office the next morning, pointing over his shoulder.

"You always leave your front door unlocked? I walked right in. You could get robbed."

He huffed out a breath. "Of what? A bunch of old furniture?"

"You might have some valuable antiques in here. Your uncle Oscar was known to drop a bundle on English furniture and rare porcelain."

Simon tamped down his irritation. "What are you doing here, Ray?"

"I was going to be in the area, so I thought I'd bring these papers over in person." He laid a slim folder on the desk then sat down.

Simon leaned back in his chair. "Why couldn't old Uncle Oscar have left me a pile of money instead of an assortment of derelict properties?"

Ray shook his head. "I told you before you came down here that finding buyers wasn't going to be easy."

He couldn't deny he'd been warned, but that wasn't

the only thing Ray had failed to warn him about. "Why didn't you tell me about the boy? I was blindsided."

Ray crossed his legs. "You mean why didn't I tell you Joy had a boy who was missing some fingers? Why should I? I don't tell people about my friend the guy with the big scar."

Heat shot up through Simon's neck. He'd walked into that one.

"How are things working out with Joy?"

He hated it when his friend was right. He chewed the inside of his lip a moment. "She's competent."

Ray chuckled. "Just what I like. A glowing report."

"She likes to hum or sing while she works. It's distracting."

"Is that it or is it because she's very pretty?"

Simon frowned at the smug look on Ray's face. "I hadn't noticed." Ray's skeptical expression challenged his words.

Joy breezed into the office. "I'm back. There was a long line at the post office. Ray. What a nice surprise."

Ray rose and gave Joy a hug like they were long-lost family. "I was hoping to see you. You look good. The job must agree with you?"

Joy glanced at him then linked her arm in Ray's. "So far. It's only day three. How's your wife liking her new job?"

Simon stared at Ray. What job? How did Joy know about Ray's wife? He searched for her name and came up empty.

"I think she was born to be a vice principal. She comes home every day happy as a lark."

"I'm so glad. I know she was worried."

"How's my little buddy, Mike?"

"Great. He loves it here. He's outside playing as soon as I bring him home from day care."

Simon watched as they chatted about Mikey, the diner and missing Miss Millie's pies. He had no idea what they were talking about. Ray turned to him.

"If you'll sign those now, I can take them with me."

"I'll see you later, Ray. I need to get back to work." She leaned close and whispered something in his ear.

Ray patted her hand. "You're welcome."

She stepped into the alcove, leaving Simon feeling like an unnecessary piece of furniture. They talked as if he wasn't even in the room. Picking up a pen, he scribbled his name on the documents, slipped them back into the folder and handed them to his friend. "I didn't know you and Joy were so close." He hated that he was curious about their friendship.

"I told you we were friends. Why else would I have recommended her for the job? She's going to be a real asset to you, pal."

Simon set his jaw. That remained to be seen. He was relieved when Ray left and he could get back to his work.

Joy walked into his office later in the morning and stopped at his desk. "Would you mind if I had a cup of that coffee? It smells really good."

"Help yourself." The coffee maker was his addition to the space. He and John had both been serious caffeine addicts. Maybe Joy was, too. He watched as she poured a cup, laced it with cream and sugar, then took a sip. She turned and smiled at him and he frowned. John never smiled. "Have you known Ray a long time?" He hadn't meant to ask but it just slipped out.

"Since I came to Blessing a few years ago. He was my best customer at Willa's Diner. A big tipper."

"And you know his wife, uh…" He searched again for her name.

"Virginia. Yes. She came to the diner a lot, too, except for when she was recovering from hip surgery." She peered at him over her cup, a frown marring her smooth brow. "I thought you and Ray were good friends."

"We are." Or at least he'd thought they were. But to be honest, he'd never asked about Ray's life or his family. They'd discussed only business and getting out from under his inheritance.

Joy held his gaze a long moment then smiled. "You get to know a lot about people working at a diner. And around town." She took her cup and went back into her alcove.

What had she meant by that? He'd clearly heard a subtle reproach in her tone. He swung his chair around and stared out the window. He didn't know anything about Ray because he'd never asked. When had he become so cut off from everyone and everything? Was that what Joy had been hinting at? That he should get out more?

He spun around again and faced the monitor. That wasn't going to happen. Certainly not here in this town, not after the way they'd treated his mother. It was the town's fault that she had died. And his uncle's. He wanted nothing to do with Blessing or the people in it.

Joy set her cup on the coaster a safe distance away from the computer then opened the files she'd been working on yesterday. Her mind refused to focus. It kept going back to Simon and his odd reaction to her greeting Ray.

He'd looked like he was stunned to find out they were friends, but Ray had gotten her the job. Simon couldn't recall the name of Ray's wife yet they were supposedly longtime friends. What was she missing?

An hour later she stood and walked into Simon's office. "Can I ask you a question?"

He looked up with a puzzled expression. "Of course."

She gauged her words, not wanting to stir up any trouble. "You want to sell all these properties you own and you want to do it quickly, right?"

"That's the plan."

"Then why don't you have a real estate agent working for you?"

Simon stared at his computer. "Ray volunteered to handle it all."

"I'm sure he's doing his best, but he doesn't have access to the Multiple Listing System or any of the marketing tools available for reaching prospective buyers. You don't just slap a for-sale sign on an old building and hope someone sees it and calls."

"Ray knows what he's doing."

Joy crossed her arms over her chest. "Oh really? How many offers have you had in the last three months?" She knew by the way Simon's eyes darkened that she'd gone too far. But the man was bullheaded for no real reason that she could see.

"The fewer people involved in my business the better."

Joy set her hands on her hips. "Isn't that backward?

The more people you have working for you the better. You want to sell things quickly, but you won't do what's necessary to make that happen." She took a deep breath and plunged on. "I could call my friend Sheila Dixon. She's the best agent in town."

"That's not much of a recommendation."

She clenched her teeth. The man was impossible. "She has offices in Hattiesburg and Biloxi, which means she has connections to bigger cities and more buyers. She just sold a cattle ranch to a guy from Oklahoma. She could speed things up for you. Isn't that what you want?"

"I'll think about it."

"Suit yourself, but the longer you think, the longer those buildings will sit on the market." She started to leave then turned back. "Of course, you could sell the bridge land to the city and that would be one less thing on your plate. And it would make the town very happy."

"This town's happiness is of no concern to me."

Joy inhaled in surprise. He might as well have tossed cold water in her face. She turned and went back to her desk. The rumors were right. The man was heartless.

She hoped she was wrong because if it were true, the future of the beloved bridge was in danger.

Saturday afternoon was fading as Mikey ran around the big backyard. Joy exhaled a contented sigh as she watched her son play. The last few days had been hectic and emotional. Getting the job, moving into the apartment and adjusting to Simon had left her exhausted. Today was her treat to herself. She'd invited Willa over to see the apartment and spend the afternoon. They'd ordered their favorite pizza then retreated to the back porch to catch up.

"So tell me. How are you getting along with our local bad-boy mystery man?"

"Okay, I guess. He's a very cold and unhappy person. I haven't seen him smile once." She decided to keep her knowledge of Simon's family to herself for the time being. "The scar isn't as bad as everyone made out. I hardly notice it anymore."

"What about the job? Do you like the work?"

Joy smiled. "I do. It's interesting and the salary will allow me to go back to college and finish my psychology degree. The most important thing is that Mikey is happy. My first paycheck is going toward replacing all the toys he lost in the fire."

Willa groaned softly and put her hand to her throat. "Oh, I'm so sorry about that."

Joy quickly reassured her. "Nonsense. That wasn't your fault. Besides, everyone got out safe and sound. The rest was only stuff. It made moving here very simple. All we had to do was unpack a plastic bag, a suitcase and a duffel. Easy-peasy."

Willa chuckled. "I guess that's a good thing. Have you been able to learn anything about what Simon plans to do with the bridge land?"

Joy's shoulders sagged. "Not specifically. He's planning on selling everything he inherited."

"Why?"

Joy took a sip of her sweet tea. "He said he wants to start a business back home."

Willa bit her lip. "What about the bridge?"

That was the million-dollar question. Joy chose her

words carefully. "He owns it, so I suppose he'll sell it, too. After all, it is part of the estate." A look of horror filled her cousin's eyes.

"He can't sell the bridge. It belongs to the town. It's ours."

Joy understood her cousin's concern. "Not really. It's only leased and that runs out late next month."

Willa bit her lip. "There's got to be something we can do. You're the vice president of the Save the Bridge Committee. Can you talk to him and make him see how important that land is?"

"I doubt that would carry much weight with Simon. I got the impression Simon doesn't like our town very much."

Willa sighed. "That's understandable, I suppose. He didn't have an easy time of it when he lived here being poor and the son of the town drunk. But, Joy, we can't sit back and do nothing. You are coming to the next committee meeting, aren't you?"

"As long as they have childcare."

"Good. Maybe we can come up with a plan."

Joy hoped for that, too, but she didn't have much faith that Simon would change his mind. He was a man on a mission and she doubted he could be stopped.

It was late Saturday afternoon when Ray called. "I have some good news. An offer has come in from an interested party in Texas. He wants the entire Afton Grove estate and the numbers are very generous."

Simon had worked with Ray long enough to read his tone. "I hear a *but* coming."

"There is. He's anxious to close the deal within the next few weeks. He wants the bridge land, too."

Simon rubbed his lower lip. The amount of the offer Ray quoted was far more than he'd expected. It would mean he could leave Blessing and get his business up and running immediately. Unfortunately, there was a hitch. "I can't sell that parcel until the lease is up next month."

"I know. I'll try to convince him to wait, but he's a bulldog. He doesn't like to be told no."

Simon fisted his free hand. He grew to hate his inheritance more each day. "I've got to unload this stuff. I want out of Blessing. I swore I'd never come back."

"You can leave. I'll handle all the details and send you the paperwork when sales are finalized."

Simon fought to quell his irritation. "You know I can't go back until I have the money to start my business. My investor is getting antsy. I'm not sure he'll hang with me until I get rid of these albatrosses. The only way I can move forward is to put Blessing behind me. There were only two things in my life I cared about, and this town took one of them and that drunken boy took the other."

"Simon, you can't keep living with this anger and hate, my friend. It'll destroy you. I know coming back here has been hard, but you were a teenager when you left. Things look different as an adult. It might help if you weren't so isolated from things. Go out, look at Blessing through new eyes. You might be surprised."

Joy had hinted at the same thing. Were they working against him? Time to end this conversation. Ray was gearing up for one of his lectures on forgiveness and Simon wasn't in the mood. "Let me know what you work out with the offer."

Simon shoved his phone away. He should never have returned to this town. He'd believed that by being here he could speed up the sale of his inheritance. Big mistake. He hadn't counted on the claws of old memories digging into him again. The resulting anger and resentment were starting to take a toll on his health. He wasn't sleeping well or eating properly, and every day he went to his office and accomplished nothing.

The upshot of it all was, Joy and Ray had a valid point. He had been keeping his distance from the town, believing he could conduct his business with Ray as his one connection. If he wanted to sell quickly, he needed a Realtor. He'd put Joy on that first thing Monday morning. She could deal with the agent and he'd keep out of it.

Simon was still rehashing what Joy and Ray had said to him later that evening. Though he didn't understand why they thought he should mingle more. He was perfectly content with the way things were. He glanced around the main parlor. He spent most of his time here. It had proved to be the most comfortable and practical, with his desk and work area at one end, and the fireplace and sitting area at the other. It was the only place he could relax and almost forget for a while where he was. He used little of the large home beyond the bedroom and bath upstairs and the kitchen and office downstairs.

Simon strolled to the window and looked out just as Mikey came running across the lawn. Joy followed behind, chasing him around and laughing. She scooped him up, swung him around, then wrapped him in a hug. Even from here Simon could see the big smiles on their faces. The happy scene should have made him smile. Instead, it scraped like sandpaper over his raw grief.

He turned away and sat at his desk, struggling to put his memories back into the locked vault where they belonged. It could have been him and his son playing and laughing on the lawn. A drunk driver on a snow-covered street sliding into an intersection had robbed him of his family. Simon clasped his hands behind his neck and prayed for the pain to stop. A fruitless gesture. His prayers hadn't been answered that night.

Nor any other.

Simon sat his coffee mug on the small table beside his chair Sunday morning then lowered himself down. He was feeling restless and he wasn't sure why. The offer on the estate was the first ray of hope he'd had since coming to this town, and he was hanging all his hopes on it going through. He'd spoken with his investor in Charlotte, and the man was willing to wait but not for long. He had several projects in the works and wasn't one to wait around and twiddle his thumbs.

Simon glanced out the window, enjoying the sway of the trees in the morning breeze. It was a beautiful Sunday morning. A church morning, his mother would have said. Mom had never missed a Sunday until she'd become ill. His wife, Holly, had been a believer, too. It had taken him a long time to reconnect with his faith, but Holly had patiently encouraged him, and one day he'd heard the Lord's voice again and returned.

A year later Holly was gone and so was his son.

Finding a reason to go back to church had been difficult. Sundays now were for running. Though he had to admit the Lord had been prodding him lately to return. He'd ignored it.

"Hi, Mr. Simon."

Simon looked over to see Mikey standing in the doorway to the office. "Hello, Mikey."

"Are you awake?"

"Uh, yes. Do you need something?" The boy had his hair combed and was wearing a pair of long pants and a polo shirt. He looked very grown-up.

He smiled and came toward him. "I want you to come to church with us this morning."

Simon blinked. This was more than a prod from the Almighty. This was a total smackdown. "That's very nice of you, Mikey, but I'm going running this morning."

"Oh. Do you have to?"

Simon tried to justify himself to the boy. "Yes, it keeps me healthy and strong." He glanced toward the door. Surely Joy would be coming after her son. She never let him far from her side. "Does your mother know you're here?"

Mikey shrugged. "Are you sure you can't come with us? Last week we learned about Zacchaeus. He was a little tiny man. This big." Mikey squinted and held his thumb and forefinger close together.

Simon placed his knuckles against his mouth to hide his smile. "Is that so?"

Mikey nodded enthusiastically. "He wanted to see Jesus but he was too little, so he climbed up in a sick tree and then Jesus said to come down so they could go eat at McDonald's."

"Mikey. What are you doing in here? You know you're not supposed to bother Mr. Simon."

"It's okay, Mom. He's already had his coffee." Mikey smiled at Simon. "Mommy doesn't like noise before she has her coffee."

Joy hurried forward. "That's enough, young man. I'm so sorry, Simon. I thought he was in the bathroom brushing his teeth."

"I'm telling him about Zacchaeus and going to eat with Jesus."

Joy frowned. "I heard and they didn't go to McDonald's."

Mikey frowned, a copy of his mother's. "Well, it could have been McDonald's."

"Did you brush your teeth?"

He lowered his head. "No, ma'am."

"Then scoot. I'll be there in a minute."

Mikey stopped at the door. "Maybe you can come next week. Mommy says that after all God does for us every day, the least we can do is go to church for an hour."

He smiled and waved goodbye and Simon waved back. The little boy was quickly worming his way into Simon's heart, no matter how hard he tried to stop it.

"I apologize."

Simon stood and waved off her concern. "It's fine. He wanted to invite me to church."

"Oh," Joy responded uncomfortably. "He loves Sunday school. He likes the Bible stories."

"I did, too. When I was a kid, Zacchaeus was one of my favorites, too. And Mikey was right, they could have gone to McDonald's." Joy laughed and he found himself captivated by the sound and the twinkle in her blue eyes. They always seemed to have sunlight behind them. Today she looked even brighter in a simple green dress that skimmed her curves.

"My son is spirited and very curious. He's itching to explore this house. He keeps sneaking off to look around." She blushed slightly. "I must admit, I'm curious, too. It's such a lovely home."

Simon intended to remind her that this was his private area, but the words he spoke surprised him. "He's welcome to explore all he wants. You, too. I never use the place except for the office and a room upstairs."

"Really? That would be wonderful. I'm afraid my son gets his curiosity from me." She moved toward the door. "Thank you. And I'm sorry about him intruding."

"Don't be." She smiled at him and caused a sudden blip in his pulse. Very strange.

"I'd better go. He's probably got toothpaste all over the bathroom."

Simon followed her to the door, watching her walk away. He'd enjoyed Mikey's visit and his imaginative version of the Zacchaeus story. He chuckled and went to the kitchen to pick up a bottle of water for his run, though for some reason, he didn't feel the need for exercise as strongly as he had earlier.

He headed out the back door and broke into a jog, humming the little song about Zacchaeus he'd learned as a child.

Monday morning was gray and dreary when Joy pulled into the small parking lot at the Blessing Bridge.

She'd dropped Mikey off at preschool a little early so she could spend a few minutes here. She needed some clarity and direction before confronting Simon today. The members of the Save the Bridge Committee had pressured her to talk to Simon and try to get an answer about his plans for the bridge land. Preparations for the bicentennial were moving ahead, but without the landmark, the celebration would be hollow.

She resisted their pleas but finally relented. Maybe she could sway him somehow. Maybe all her hard work would nudge him toward helping Blessing. A small plaque marked the entrance to a narrow path into the woods. *The Blessing Bridge. A place of hope and peace. Lift your cares to the Lord with a sincere heart and a humble spirit and return renewed.*

Her heart rate slowed and her tension eased the moment she stepped through the trees and onto the winding path to the bridge. Despite its run-down state, there was a sense of peace and tranquility here. She believed the Lord answered His children's prayers. Whether they were answered more frequently here was debatable. What the bridge did offer was a serene location to lift up those prayers. Sometimes, even the worshipful atmosphere of church could be distracting. But here, there was nothing to intrude beyond the rustle of the leaves and the sweet songs of birds.

Joy stood at the middle of the bridge leaning against the railing and allowing the quiet to seep into her heart. Her prayers today were ones of gratitude for her job, her family and her blessings. She also prayed for the right words to approach Simon. She wanted to see the grounds restored and beautified, and she feared that if Simon sold it, the very fabric of Blessing would be shredded.

Her nerves were quivering as she entered the office a short while later. What was the worst that could happen? She'd be out of work again.

Simon glanced up as she entered. He looked unusually pleasant today. He really was a handsome man when he wasn't scowling. She stopped and stared. His whole face looked different. The scar was still there and that one wave in his nearly black hair still dipped down, but the darkness in his eyes had lightened. Even the cotton shirt he wore was a brighter color. Her pulse skipped. Should she be alarmed or delighted?

"Good morning, Joy."

"Simon. Has something happened?"

He grinned and leaned back in his chair. "Yes. I have an offer on the estate. A developer in Fort Worth wants the whole thing. And at a very generous price."

Not what she'd wanted to hear first thing today. It was the worst possible news. If the offer for Afton Grove went through, the city could lose the bridge forever. Someone who wanted three hundred acres probably had big development plans in mind. Something like that could destroy the quaint small-town appeal of Blessing. "Oh. That's good news." The words wanted to stick in her throat.

"Very good news."

"And the bridge land?" She'd wanted to ease her way into discussing the bridge, but she didn't have that luxury now. She held her breath.

Simon didn't look up. "It's part of the package. Provided the prospective buyer will wait until the lease agreement expires."

Joy wanted to cry. Why would Simon deliberately ruin Blessing? Maybe he didn't understand the significance of his inheritance? "You know that the Blessing Bridge is the very heart of this town."

He met her gaze. "I do."

Joy struggled to understand. "Then why are you thinking of selling it? Simon, the bicentennial is less than a year away. Events have already begun. One each month. Everyone in the town is involved. The bicentennial poster is on display everywhere and it's being shared on social media every day. Did you know that a local woman designed the poster? And there's a book, a history of Blessing has been written and will be in stores next month."

"That's not my concern."

"Well, it should be. This is your hometown."

He shook his head, his jaw rigid. "Not my hometown. Just the place I used to live."

The hard tone in his voice was disturbing and raised her defenses. "Blessing is a wonderful place to live. The people here are caring and generous. They treated us like family when we came here. Mikey and I desperately needed that after my life fell apart."

Simon held her gaze, his eyes dark. "That might be your story but it's not mine."

Joy's frustration mounted. "If you sell the bridge land, it could be the death of this town. That bridge has been the symbol of Blessing for decades. It's a landmark, a tourist destination. Meridian has its historic

Dentzel Carousel and we have the Blessing Bridge. Think about the long-range ramifications."

"I am. The ramifications if I can't unload these useless properties."

"Why don't you donate the land to the town permanently?" It was the hoped-for solution.

Simon stood and shook his head. "Out of the question. I need every penny if I'm going to go home and start my business."

Joy searched frantically for another tack. "What if you sold the bridge to the town? Then we'd have the landmark and you'd have your money."

Simon's expression changed. He stared at her as if trying to understand. "Why is this so important? It's just an old bridge. It has no power."

"Maybe not, but it has offered hope to thousands of people over the years. Please, Simon, at least consider selling it. That way everyone would win."

Simon picked up his cell phone and pressed the buttons. "I have some calls to make and I'm sure you have work to do." He spun his chair around and faced the window.

She'd been dismissed. She went into her office, troubled by Simon's feelings toward Blessing. She loved everything about the small town. Was his troubled childhood to blame for such deep resentment or was there something more? She could only pray that Simon would consider her suggestion to sell the land to the city. It was the perfect solution.

Chapter Three

Wednesday morning, Joy approached Simon's office with her stomach churning. She glanced down at her son, gently smoothing his hair. When she'd taken this job, she'd failed to factor in unexpected surprises, like a car that wouldn't start. Now she had to approach him first thing today for a favor. Gathering her courage, she stepped into the room.

After a week and a half on the job, she'd found her rhythm and was enjoying the work. Simon had been less intimidating by the day, but he was hardly the kind of boss she could tease or chitchat with. He was particularly grumpy this week because he hadn't heard from the Texas developer yet. He wouldn't welcome this interruption.

"Hey, Mr. Simon."

Joy hushed her son and took his hand. Simon looked up with his usual deep scowl. She smiled and took a step farther into the room, "I'm sorry to bother you but I need a favor." She braced for a curt reply.

"Our car is sick," Mikey announced happily. "It goes clicky-clicky instead of vroom."

Simon studied them, his brown eyes reflecting his puzzlement. "I see."

Joy breathed a little easier. His tone wasn't edged with the irritation she'd expected. Instead he'd spoken in a calm, curious manner. She plunged ahead. "I was wondering if you could drive Mikey to school this morning. I know you have a lot for me to do, but I can't work if he's with me. My cousin Willa is normally my backup but she's out of town."

Simon held her gaze a long moment then stood.

"On one condition. You come with me to the Mc-Cray building after we drop Mikey off. I'm meeting a potential buyer and I'd like your input."

She blinked. Not what she'd expected. "Okay. Of course. Thank you."

Mikey pulled from her grasp and approached Simon as he came around his desk. "Are we going to ride in your big truck?"

Simon looked down at her son, his expression softening. "Yes, we are."

Mikey jumped up. "Super cool. I love trucks."

After transferring the child seat from her old car to the shiny new truck and instructing her boss on the proper way to install it, Joy settled in while Mikey chattered from the back seat.

"I really appreciate this. Mikey loves his preschool."

"I'll need directions."

"Yes, of course. Turn left at the next street." She watched Simon out of the corner of her eye. He drove with an easy, relaxed confidence, a departure from his usual tense, scowling attitude. It changed his whole demeanor and softened the sharp angles of his face. He really was a handsome man. With the angry scowl missing, he could easily be a heartbreaker. The scar only added a roguish quality to his swashbuckling good looks. It was easy to imagine him with an eye patch, a gold earring and a cutlass in his hand. She swiftly squashed those thoughts. "That's the school on the right." Joy quickly unbuckled her son, handed him over to the teacher's assistant and kissed him goodbye.

Back in the truck, she smiled at Simon. He never smiled back except for an occasional small grin with Mikey, but she was determined to persist. That was a sight she'd like to see. She had a feeling his smile would melt a woman's heart like a blowtorch.

"How are you going to pick him up after school?"

"Willa should be home by then."

"Let me know if you need a chauffeur again."

Speechless, she studied his profile. Was he joking or being sarcastic? Maybe he wasn't as cold as she'd first thought. "I'm not sure how I can help you at the McCray building."

"By providing a different perspective." Simon pulled the truck into one of the angled parking slots in the front of the empty building then got out and came around to open her door.

"I didn't know you'd found a buyer."

"Your friend Sheila called me last night."

She grinned. "I told you she was good."

Joy glanced up at the three-story structure. The Mc-Cray building was one of the oldest in the downtown area and had housed the first department store in Blessing. Now, however, it was one of the few eyesores on the charming square. Her burn-scarred former home and diner was the other. At least work had started on that. Willa would be able to open again before long.

Joy walked with Simon along the side of the building. A faded sign from a previous occupant was still visible on the gray walls. A short, rotund man waited at the rear door. Simon greeted him, introduced him as Hiram Green, then unlocked the door and stepped inside. She'd been curious about this place since she'd arrived in Blessing. Her imagination took flight as she scanned the vast interior. She could see it being transformed into a variety of businesses. Hopefully, the interested party had similar plans. Blessing could always benefit from new commerce. She prayed she could convince Simon of that, and the importance of the beloved landmark, too.

She was a firm believer in saving the town's historic structures.

Simon walked a few paces behind Joy and Mr. Green, marveling at how easily she handled the meeting. After only a short time on the job, Joy had brought a new atmosphere to his office. She'd learned the ropes quickly and was always thorough and prompt. He'd even grown used to her soft humming as she worked. Some days she hummed slow, sweet tunes. Other times happy, upbeat songs.

He'd suspected the song reflected whatever suited her mood that day. He often wondered where that good mood came from. Despite losing her job and home in the fire, and being a single parent of a little boy with a disability, she could still find something good in everything.

He doubted if she could find any good in him.

Now, as he walked through the old building, Simon had very little to do or say. Joy had greeted the prospective buyer with a warm smile and immediately began extolling the possibilities of the site. All he saw was a vacant, cavernous space. Joy saw visions.

An hour later, Simon shook hands with Mr. Green, his hopes rising. The man had seemed genuinely interested and Joy's enthusiastic comments had helped. He locked the door and started back to the truck, Joy at his side. She smiled at him.

"That went well, don't you think?"

He nodded. "Thanks to you."

"Me? What did I do?"

Did she really not know? "You made the place sound like the greatest business opportunity since Microsoft." She giggled and his pulse jumped.

"Well, it could be. Blessing is low on housing. Turning the upper floors into lofts or small apartments would be a boost to the economy. The bicentennial will bring in new residents, even if it's only temporary, but some of them might stay on. Blessing is a wonderful place to live."

Simon didn't respond. No need to kill her good mood with facts about the idyllic town she loved. Though he wondered what she saw in the place that he never had.

"Simon? Simon Baker? Is that you?"

He stopped as an older woman approached, a warm smile on her face.

"I knew it was you. I heard you were back in Blessing. I'm so glad you came home. Your mama would be so happy."

It took Simon a moment to recognize the woman. "Hello, Mrs. Doyle."

Her smile widened. "Oh, you remember me. Imagine that after all this time. Your mama was such a dear person. I still miss her. What brings you back here?"

She had to be the only resident of Blessing who didn't know. "I inherited the Afton Grove estate."

Her smile faded. "Oh yes. I did hear that. I'm sure that will be a challenge for you." She patted his arm. "But your mama always said you had a good heart. I tried so hard to help but, well, you know how hard it was."

She looked at Joy. "Oh. You're the waitress from the diner, aren't you? I was so sad to hear about the fire. I miss Willa's good food." She turned her gaze back on him. "I'd better be getting along. You be sweet now. I look forward to seeing you again. Welcome home."

Simon's jaw started to ache from clenching his teeth. He took Joy's arm and steered her firmly toward the truck.

"What's wrong?"

He climbed behind the wheel and started the engine, barely keeping to the speed limit as he drove back to the house. Thankfully, Joy didn't press him for an explanation. He needed time to cool off.

He pulled to a stop at the front of the house and killed the engine. He should never have come back to Blessing.

"I'm sorry."

Joy's soft words pierced his irritation. "Excuse me?"

"I'm sorry for whatever pain that woman dredged up."

Simon met her gaze. Something in her blue eyes drew him. He never talked about the past to anyone. Not even his wife. But here, in the quiet confines of the truck, he felt an unfamiliar need to share. Why Joy should bring this out in him was a mystery.

"She used to be a friend of my mother's. They did church work together. My mom considered Violet Doyle her best friend. What a joke."

"Why? Did something happen?"

Simon searched for a place to begin. "My mother got sick. She needed help. My dad was always too busy holding down a stool at the Gator Bar."

"And Mrs. Doyle helped?"

"No. No one did." He fought to keep the harsh tone out of his voice. "My family was from the wrong side of the tracks, so we didn't deserve help. I don't know what she was talking about. She never helped."

"What about county services, or people from the church? Wasn't there someone you could turn to for assistance?"

Simon gripped the steering wheel. "You mean like family? A wealthy family member who could have gotten medicines or arranged hospital care?" Simon inhaled a calming breath. Reliving that time wasn't easy. "I went to see my distant uncle, the great Oscar Templeton of Afton Grove. I knew we were related, even though we were never acknowledged. I thought I could convince him to help us since Mom was so sick."

"But he didn't."

Simon glanced at her and the understanding in her blue eyes encouraged him to continue. "No. He wouldn't even come to the door to speak to me. His housekeeper sent me away. Mom died a few days later. Where was Violet Doyle then?"

Joy's small hand covered his. "I'm so sorry, Simon. That must have been heartbreaking for a young boy."

He would have used a harsher word. "We left town after that. Dad dropped me off with my older sister and disappeared. I lived with Hannah and her husband until I went to college."

"So is this why you don't like being in Blessing? Too many bad memories?"

Her question made him realize he'd shared much more than he intended. He opened the truck door. "We need to get to work. Thanks for listening."

"Anytime, Simon. It helps to share with people who care."

Simon met her gaze. Did she care? Why? They barely knew each other. But he couldn't deny that Joy had a way about her that invited others to share their concerns without fear of being judged or betrayed. The way the people of Blessing had betrayed his family.

Simon opened the front door, catching Joy's gaze. "Thanks for your help with Mr. Green. You have a knack for creating enthusiasm in people. I might put you in charge of promoting my other properties."

She smiled and his pulse did that odd skip again. "I don't know about that, but it might be fun to try. Sometimes you have to paint a picture for people before they can see the potential." She shrugged. "I have a good imagination."

Simon followed her into the house, vowing to make arrangements to have Joy's car repaired.

It was the least he could do for a valuable employee.

* * *

Joy headed toward her alcove when they returned to the office. The tour of the McCray building, while exhilarating, had put her behind on her regular tasks. If she worked through lunch, she could get caught up. Trouble was, she couldn't get Simon off her mind. Learning about his childhood in Blessing explained a lot.

After the treatment he'd received, it was no wonder he resented the town and everyone in it. Still, she found it hard to believe that everyone in Blessing had turned their back on Simon and his mother. Mrs. Doyle seemed genuinely glad to see him and regretful of her inability to help his mother. Was there more to the story? It wasn't only his mother that Simon had lost. He'd lost his wife and child, too.

It was late afternoon when Simon appeared at her desk. She smiled, eager to thank him for arranging for a new battery to be put in her car, but the look on his face sent her pulse racing. He looked more grumpy than usual. "Did something happen?"

"I just got a call from Ray. The Texas deal fell through. The developer didn't want to wait, so he's moved on to another project."

"Oh, I'm so glad." Too late she realized her mistake. His dark scowl sent her heart into her throat. This might be bad news for Simon, but it was joyous news for her and Blessing. "I'm sorry. I know how much you were counting on this offer."

Simon nodded. "And I know how much you were hoping it would fail."

She blushed. "No, I mean, yes. I won't deny that the

bridge means a great deal to me. It means a lot to everyone in Blessing."

He shoved his hands into his pockets, "I'm back to square one. I'll never get out of here. I'm a pilot, not a property manager."

Joy searched his gaze for an explanation. "A pilot?" She'd never considered what he'd done for a living before coming to Blessing. "What kind of business are you planning on starting?"

"An air charter service. But it's an expensive proposition. I need the profits from this inheritance to get things off the ground."

Her hopes began to fade. She'd assumed Simon wanted to sell for simple revenge, but he had a mission. That changed things. People didn't turn away from that kind of goal. They only dug in their heels. "I didn't know."

"I was a pilot in the air force for ten years. It's what I love to do. After I separated from the service, I flew a corporate jet for a company in Charlotte."

Joy's heart thudded. "You lived in Charlotte? North Carolina?"

"Yes, why?"

"I lived there, too, before coming here to Blessing."

Simon nodded in acknowledgment. "It's a great place. We… I liked living there." He sighed then turned to go. "Let's hope Mr. Green decides soon. This inheritance is becoming a curse."

Joy bit her lip as Simon walked away, anxiety churning in her stomach. He'd lived in Charlotte before moving here. Her gaze fell on the paperwork on her desk and Simon's name printed in bold type at the top. That sense of familiarity fluttered in her mind again. What was happening? Pressure started to build in her skull. Why did his name plague her?

There had to be an explanation. Had they met sometime when they were living in North Carolina? Was that why his name had triggered a memory? Unlikely, since she'd been alone after Chad had walked out, and her social life had consisted of work and church. Besides, with his dark good looks and that scar, a man like Simon wouldn't slip her mind. She tried to remember the people her husband had known, but she couldn't recall anyone named Simon. It was a coincidence, that was all. There had to be dozens of Simon Bakers in Charlotte.

Joy rubbed her temple as the headache deepened. The doctors had warned her that stress could trigger them, and it had been a very stressful day, starting with the tour of the McCray building. Meeting Viola Doyle and learning about Simon's past had stirred her compassion for her boss. The collapse of the Texas deal had given her new hope for the bridge, but discovering Simon had lived in her former hometown had pushed everything else aside. Retrieving a bottle of pain medicine from her purse, she swallowed two. Thankfully, the prescription always worked quickly.

By the time she was ready to leave for the day, however, her headache had eased only slightly. The possibility of losing the bridge overrode all other concerns. She decided to make a stab at ending one of her worries.

Simon glanced up as she approached, still wearing his usual scowl. Now might not be the best time but she needed to know his intentions. "With this change in plans, I was wondering if you'd thought any more about selling the bridge land to the city?"

His expression grew even darker. "No. That's not at the top of my list."

"Of course. I understand." She exhaled and nodded. She'd have nothing to report at the next committee meeting, which meant she'd be under the gun again.

Back at her desk, she closed her computer and neatly stacked the papers and slipped them into the to-do tray. Simon's name on the folder caused a flash of pain in her skull. Her heartbeat quickened. Why was this happening? She tried to connect the wisp of the past with Simon but came up empty again. Maybe she was imagining the whole thing. She forced the notion back into the far recesses of her mind. She was growing fearful of some vague impression that had no substance.

But the sensation refused to stay silent and she had a strong feeling that something about his name was important.

Very important.

Chapter Four

Simon ended his evening run at the front of the house, wanting to avoid any chance encounter with Joy. He wasn't ready to deal with seeing the disappointment about the bridge in her blue eyes again. He also knew her well enough now to know she'd keep pressing him to come up with a price for the land. Maybe if he priced it high enough, the town would forget the whole idea.

His conscience stirred, reminding him of how helpful Joy had been today with Mr. Green. He'd called while Simon was on his run to ask a few more questions. His continued interest in the building was all because of Joy. It was clear she was an optimistic woman, always looking at the bright side and emotionally attached to people and things. She'd found happiness in this town and she thought he should, too. That would never happen.

After a quick shower, Simon went to the kitchen and fixed a sandwich. He wasn't really hungry but it gave him something to do while his mind was churning. Losing the Texas buyer was a big blow to his plans.

Picking up his plate and glass, he headed to the office. He ate all his meals here. Except for once a week when he and Ray went to Hattiesburg for a steak dinner. Simon avoided Blessing. He didn't want to deal with the stares and curious looks, nor did he want to run into more Violas. It only drew attention to the fact that he didn't belong here and wasn't welcome.

His gaze drifted to the alcove where Joy worked. The space felt dull and empty without her sunny presence. Simon killed that train of thought. He was tired and not thinking clearly. Picking up his sandwich again, he swiveled his chair and looked out the window. His heart skipped a beat. Joy was in the yard assembling a small soccer goal. Mikey was hunkered down, watching with eager anticipation on his face. The moment Joy finished, he picked up the small ball and kicked it toward the goal, lifting his arms in triumph as it rolled into the net.

Simon stood and moved closer to the window, ignoring the voice in his head scolding him for watching his tenants. He smiled. Mikey was a remarkable kid. Joy was right. There was no reason to feel sorry for the little guy. Mikey caught sight of him and waved. Simon quickly stepped back from the window, his cheeks warming. That was what he got for spying.

He turned away. Watching them together had filled him with an unfamiliar desire to go into the yard and kick the ball to Mikey and make him laugh. Simon returned to his chair and stared at his sandwich. He'd always enjoyed eating alone, but something about the new tenants made him realize how isolated he'd become. After shoving the plate away, he moved to his favorite chair and sat down, then stretched his legs out. His mood was quickly turning dark.

"Mr. Simon."

Simon jerked his head toward the office door. Mikey stood there with a big smile on his face.

"We're having spaghetti with meatballs and crunchy bread for supper. My favorite."

Simon quickly checked his surprise. "That sounds delicious."

"Can you come and eat with us? Mommy said we have plenty for everybody."

The knot in Simon's chest eased at the child's thoughtfulness. He was tempted to accept the invitation. The thought of homemade spaghetti was more appetizing than a cold ham sandwich. "That's very nice of you, Mikey, but I've already eaten. Maybe next time."

Mikey's smile faded. "Okay, but I really wanted you to come."

The boy's disappointment surprised him. "Why's that?"

"Because I like you." His expression grew serious. "And because people with big boo-boos need friends."

A huge knot formed in Simon's throat. Before he could speak, Mikey spun and dashed off. Simon could hear his feet tapping on the wood floors as he ran back toward the apartment. Simon dragged a hand over his jaw. Out of the mouths of babes. He needed friends. He needed more than this house. Joy and Mikey were nudging him to climb out of his dark cave and rejoin the world.

Unfortunately, knowing what he should do and finding the strength to do it were two different things. He wasn't ready to forgive or to forget. He'd lost too much. He couldn't afford to get close to them.

Simon trailed his finger along the raised skin on his cheek. Mikey hadn't been upset by it. Neither had his mother. They'd treated it matter-of-factly. His heart skipped a beat as he thought of the little boy's hand. He didn't seem ashamed or embarrassed at all. He'd behaved as if it didn't matter. Maybe it didn't.

He stood just as Joy hurried into the room, looking flushed and upset. In her faded jeans and loose shirt, she looked more like a teenager than a mom.

"I'm so sorry. Mikey asked if we had plenty of food and I said yes not realizing he would come over here and bother you."

"It wasn't a bother. He invited me to dinner."

"Oh, yes, well, of course you're welcome. I just didn't think you'd… That is, I figured you'd…"

Simon held up a hand. "I turned him down. No need to feel obligated."

"Good. I mean, you're welcome anytime. We always have more than enough."

He grinned. Her befuddled state was charming. "It was very kind of Mikey to invite me. He's a great little guy." He slipped his hands into his pockets. "My son would have been three. He's giving me a glimpse of what my life could have been."

Joy's eyes quickly filled with sympathy and understanding. "I'm so sorry. If it would help, I'll keep Mikey away."

"No." He shook his head. "Nothing can change the past or bring back what I lost."

"I do understand, Simon." She came toward him.

"My life changed without warning, too. My husband couldn't handle Mikey's hand, and after my car accident, he couldn't handle my recovery. One morning he just walked out. I never saw him again."

Simon looked away, tamping down the anger her revelation had triggered. How could anyone walk away from their family? Simon would give anything to have his back. Joy might understand to a point but not the full scope of his loss.

"It was a stupid, reckless driver. A moment of distraction or drunken fog and my world ended. And I'll never forgive him." He heard the anger and bitterness in his voice and winced. He met her gaze and saw the depth of her compassion. She'd comfort him if he allowed it. She would wrap her arms around him and ease the pain. He broke eye contact. That could never happen.

Joy lightly placed her hand on his upper arm. "Simon, no one can live with anger and resentment all the time. It turns to poison in your system and destroys all your joy and hope."

The touch of her fingers was warm through the fabric of his shirt. He looked into her eyes and saw affection. Did she like him? Was her compassion genuine? Why? He hadn't been particularly friendly since her arrival.

"I appreciate your concern but you have no understanding of the situation at all." He didn't realize how harshly he'd spoken until he saw Joy flinch. The tenderness in her eyes died, leaving a sharp splinter in his chest. Her chin lifted and her mouth pressed into a tight line.

"I'm sure you're correct. After all, no one else in the world has ever had a tragedy in their life."

She whirled and walked out. Simon ran a hand down the back of his neck. He should be relieved that Joy had been chased off. So why did he feel like he'd just trampled a pretty flower?

Joy carried a tray of refreshments out onto the back porch of the apartment the next evening and placed it on the small table in front of the two rockers. Willa smiled and took a couple of cookies from the plate. "These smell delicious. I love your sugar cookies."

Joy chuckled and sat down. "I know. So does Mikey. He's already had more than he should have. I'm hoping he'll run off some of that energy." Her gaze followed her son as he ran and kicked the soccer ball.

"You may have an athlete on your hands. That boy never stops moving."

"He invited Simon to dinner last night."

Willa's eyes widened. "Oh? What did Simon say?"

"He turned him down. Mikey keeps going to see him. He says they are friends."

"How does Simon feel about that?"

"I don't know. He told me his son would have been three years old if he had lived. It broke my heart. Can you imagine how hard it is for him to have Mikey around all the time? I offered to keep Mikey away but he said it wouldn't change anything."

Willa sighed. "I can't image losing a child."

Joy had told her cousin about Simon losing his family. "I wish you could have heard him. He's so angry and bitter about the person who was behind the wheel. It's frightening. I wish I could help him somehow."

"I know, but the best thing you can do is pray for him."

"I know." Joy plucked a cookie from the plate and took a bite. She knew prayer was the answer but sometimes it didn't feel like enough. "I can't shake the feeling there's another Simon hiding behind that gruff exterior."

"You may be right. Unfortunately, grief is something everyone has to work through on their own. I know firsthand how hard that can be."

Joy nodded. Willa's husband had died of an infection several years ago. Owning the diner had given her cousin a purpose and a direction. Simon had lost his whole world. She had lost a husband, but she'd had Mikey to be her reason for moving forward. What did Simon have?

The question rolled around in the back of her mind all night. Her heart ached for him. She wondered how strong his faith was and if it had sustained him through his ordeal. The few comments he'd made about the Blessing Bridge led to her to suspect he was shaking his fist at the Lord instead of taking comfort in His grace. She drifted off to sleep searching for some way to help Simon get past his anger and into the acceptance phase of grief.

Joy came wide-awake, sitting upright and staring at the foot of her bed. There was no one there. She'd been dreaming. Her heart pounded violently in her chest, and she was drenched in sweat and gulping in deep breaths. She closed her eyes, trying to calm her nerves and let the fear that had gripped her dissipate.

Lying back down, she let her mind replay the dream. A police officer had been standing near the foot of her bed. He was speaking but she couldn't make out the words. Placing her palms over her face, she willed the image to disappear. She peeked at the clock. Two a.m. The terror slowly started to wash away, but the vision of the officer lingered. What did it mean? Why had it frightened her so strongly? Rolling onto her side, she then tugged the covers up to her chin and drew up her knees. What had triggered it? She tried to recall the accident but all she could conjure up was a blurred picture of the hospital room and shadowy figures moving around.

Frustrated, she rolled over and tried to think of something else, but a headache exploded in her skull. She got up, took her meds, then crawled back into bed. Thankfully, the prescription did its job and she was soon too drowsy to stay awake and drifted off to sleep.

Simon awoke Sunday morning more rested than he'd felt in weeks. Sheila Dixon had called last night with an official offer from Mr. Green for the McCray building, renewing Simon's hope for unloading his unwanted bequest. Ray had predicted Joy would be a blessing and she had, and he intended to tell her so first thing Monday morning. Today, however, he was taking a break. For the first time since he'd returned to Blessing, he would set aside all the tension and frustration over selling his properties and simply relax.

Fixing another cup of coffee, Simon strode toward the front door and the rockers on the porch.

"Hi, Mr. Simon."

He glanced over his shoulder to see Mikey hurrying toward him. "Good morning. Where are you heading?" The boy was cute as a button and never failed to bring a smile to Simon's face.

"Mommy and me are going to church. You want to come with us?"

The invitation caught him off guard, sending an uncomfortable tremor along his nerves. "No. Not today." The boy's expression revealed his disappointment.

"Mikey. Where are you?"

"Coming." He smiled and waved. "I'll see you later. Bye."

Simon watched the child disappear down the hall, marveling at his persistent happy mood. Carrying his coffee to the porch, he stood at the rail watching as Joy's car appeared from the side of the house and moved down the long driveway on their way to Sunday services.

Church. He hadn't been since his wife died. Ray kept asking him to come with him, but Simon wasn't on speaking terms with the Lord and he didn't want to spend any time in His house listening to words that felt hollow after losing his family. But Mikey's sweet invitation refused to leave his thoughts and he found himself getting dressed and driving downtown to the historic Blessing Community Church.

As if drawn by a magnet, his gaze found Joy and Mikey the moment he stepped into the sanctuary. He took a seat in the last pew for an easy exit. His tenants were seated midway down the aisle but somehow Mikey spotted him immediately and got on his knees in the pew and waved. His big smile and sparkling eyes were impossible to resist and Simon smiled and waved back. His mother nudged him to turn around and sit down, but he pointed at him. She glanced over her shoulder and froze. Her surprise quickly melted into a smile, as if she was not only glad to see him but pleased he was in attendance.

Was she? More important, why was she so determined to change his opinion of Blessing? What difference did it make to her how he felt?

The opening hymn shifted his thoughts and he focused on the service, with an occasional glance at Joy and Mikey. The little boy didn't look back at him again, creating a strange sense of disappointment in Simon's chest. When Reverend Miller began the benediction, Simon slipped out and headed toward his car, only to be stopped by someone shouting his name. He turned as Ray came hurrying up.

"Has the earth stopped moving? Has the world shut down?" He smiled and lightly punched Simon's arm. "Something monumental must have occurred to get Hermit Baker out of his cave and into church."

Simon nodded, acknowledging the teasing from his friend. "Nothing has happened. I just felt like coming today. It's not a big deal."

Ray's expression sobered. "Simon. It's me you're talking to. I know all your reasons for staying away from the Lord. So what's changed? Does this have anything to do with the offer on the McCray building? Great news, huh? Full price, quick sale. That's one less thing you have to deal with. Congrats, buddy. How did this come about?"

Simon rubbed his upper lip, gauging how much he

wanted to share. "Joy. I took her along when I met with Mr. Green. She—" he shook his head, still marveling at how she'd charmed the man "—convinced him that it was the opportunity of a lifetime."

A sly smile spread across Ray's craggy features. "I knew it. I told you she'd be a blessing, didn't I?"

"She was this time."

"Good." Ray glanced over his shoulder when his wife called to him. He saluted and walked off.

"Mr. Simon. Mr. Simon."

Mikey ran up to him all smiles. "I'm glad you came to church."

"I am, too." He looked at Joy as she came toward him at a slower pace. She was looking very feminine in dark slacks and a lacey top. "Good morning."

She smiled. "Did you enjoy the sermon?"

Simon searched for a response. He'd found it difficult to pay attention to the preacher. His thoughts kept drifting to his tenants. "I did." Joy's skeptical smile raised a splinter of guilt in his chest. He was lying in the church yard.

"Maybe next week's service will hold your attention."

Simon tugged at his ear. Joy looked past him, a warm smile spreading across her face. "Arlo."

A teenage boy came toward them. "Hello, Miss Joy. Hi, squirt." He patted Mikey on top of his head.

"Simon, this is Arlo Gayton. He was one of our bus-boys at Willa's Diner."

The teenager shook Simon's hand, staring at his scar. "What happened?"

Joy touched the young man's arm to draw his attention from Simon. "How's your gram doing? I saw on the prayer chain that she'd fallen and fractured her wrist."

"Yes, ma'am. She's doing okay but she misses her baking." He waved at a group of boys who were calling to him. "See ya later. Nice to meet you, sir."

Simon watched him run off to join his friends. "He seems like a nice kid."

"He is, and a hard worker, too. His grandmother, Millie Gayton, baked our pies. She supplied most of the restaurants in Blessing. The diner was her biggest client until the fire put them both out of work. It's been hard for them."

"I'm sure something will turn up." He chose to ignore the teen's reaction to his scar.

"I hope so. Millie is one of the dearest women in town."

Simon puzzled over how Joy appeared to know everyone and their situations.

Joy smiled and took Mikey's hand. "We're meeting Willa for lunch. Would you like to join us?"

The invite caught him by surprise and he responded automatically. "No. I have plans. But thank you."

She started to walk off then turned and looked back. "It was good to see you here this morning. There's hope for you yet."

Simon watched her walk toward her car, puzzling over her remark. Hope for what?

He sometimes thought Joy spoke a totally different language. He found himself wishing he'd accepted her offer to have lunch.

* * *

Joy loved Monday mornings. Most people hated them, but she liked the anticipation of what the week would bring. She hit the send button on the email she'd just written then leaned back in her chair. Simon had been out of the office, which had allowed her to get caught up on her work. After seeing him at church yesterday, she'd been conjuring up all kinds of reasons for him changing his mind and attending services. He'd looked different and very handsome in gray trousers and a crisp white shirt. Whatever his motivation, she was pleased. Maybe it signaled a crack in his hard shell.

She glanced up when he appeared in front of her desk later that morning. He had an unusually pleasant expression on his face. He stared at her a long moment, making her uneasy. "Is something wrong?" He almost smiled, catching her off guard.

"Mr. Green wants to buy the McCray building. He called me Saturday night."

It took a moment for the news to register. She smiled. "That's wonderful. Congratulations."

"He said your enthusiasm and ideas for the space convinced him he could make a nice profit and help the town along the way."

Joy blinked. "Oh. That was very kind of him."

Simon slipped his hands into his pockets. "He's right. You're a valuable asset. I appreciate your help."

She tilted her head. "Thank you. But I'm not going to change my mind about the bridge."

Simon held her gaze for a brief moment and she thought she saw a smile lighten his dark eyes. Then he shook his head, turned and walked away.

Joy grinned then returned her focus to the computer. Well, well. A sale, church and now a compliment. What other surprises did her boss have in store?

She didn't have long to speculate. After carrying her lunch out to the back porch of her apartment, she took a seat in the rocker just as the riding mower whizzed past, filling the air with the sweet scent of freshly cut grass. It stopped suddenly and turned around. The rider smiled and waved at her.

"Arlo! What are you doing here?" She stood and went to the railing.

"Mr. Simon hired me to take care of his yard. He pays real good, too."

She was well acquainted with Simon's generosity. "That's good news, Arlo. I'm so glad. I'm sure your gram is happy, too."

"Yes, ma'am. Now she won't have to worry about the bills while she recovers."

"This job won't interfere with your schooling, will it?"

Arlo shook his head. "No, ma'am. Mr. Simon said I can work whenever I need to. As long as I get the work done. Today was a teacher workday, so I figured I'd get a jump on things. I'd better get back at it."

Simon was behind his desk when she went back to the office after lunch. He didn't look up when she approached. "I see you have a new employee."

He raised his head, brows knitted together. "What?"

"I saw Arlo mowing the lawn. Weren't you happy with Grass Masters?"

Simon avoided her gaze as if embarrassed. "No."

"So you decided a teenage boy would be a better solution than a professional lawn service?"

Simon rubbed his forehead then peered at her over his fingers. "The kid needed a job."

Joy smiled. "Yes, he did. Thank you. He'll work hard for you. What made you decide to do this?"

"I told you. He needed a job. And I didn't like the looks of those boys he was with at church."

Joy nodded. "Neither did I. Let's hope filling his extra hours with honest work will keep him too busy to get into trouble." She studied her boss a moment. "Arlo could use a mentor like you. Someone to give him advice and keep him on the straight and narrow."

Simon shook his head. "Not my job. I'm not a counselor."

Joy smiled down at him. He had his head bowed, avoiding her gaze. "You're a good man, Simon Baker, even if you don't want anyone to know." He glanced up and she saw something flash behind his eyes. It came and went too quickly for her to discern the emotion before he raised his shield and broke eye contact. Her heart fluttered with delight at this new glimpse of the part of him he kept buried so deeply. Her hope for him rose every day.

"You need to get with Sheila and work out the details of this sale to Mr. Green."

Joy's hopeful mood plummeted. "Isn't that your job? It's your property."

"And I'm making it your responsibility."

Her patience was worn thin. She didn't understand this man at all. "Why do you keep everyone at arm's length? Ray is your only friend and you don't talk to him very often. You don't even talk to me and Mikey much and we live here in the house. If you'd make yourself more available, get out and mingle, you might open up new avenues for selling things."

Simon's jaw worked so rapidly Joy feared it might come loose. His eyes were dark and flashing. "I should think the answer would be obvious."

Joy couldn't believe what she was hearing. Was the man really that sensitive? "Is that what this is about? Your scar? That's a sorry excuse, Simon. It's the initial surprise of seeing the scar that startles people. After that, it becomes part of the person and they don't even think about it anymore. I didn't see anyone running away in terror at church yesterday."

"You don't know what you're talking about."

"Oh really? I think I know all about it. I have a son with a birth defect. We face stares and questions every time we go out. The moment people see his hand, they get that pitiful look on their faces or they turn away in disgust. But Mikey doesn't run away. He keeps moving forward, and from where I stand, he's a braver man at five than you are at whatever age you are. At least he's trying. You're just hiding in an old house looking at life through peepholes. Your isolation only makes speculation grow."

She gasped and covered her mouth. What had she been thinking? She couldn't talk to her boss that way. Horrified, she closed her eyes and waited for the pink slip to be hurled her way.

Simon's jaw clenched. "It's not my scar that people stare at. It's my history that turns them away. No one wants to see the town bad boy return as lord of the manor."

She hadn't expected that. It had never occurred to her. "Oh. I see. Well, then you need to prove them wrong. Be a benevolent lord. Help the town, give back. If you continue to hide in this house and play the recluse, all you're doing is making the gossip and speculation worse. Participate. Connect. Let people get used to seeing you and realize you're not going to destroy their town."

"Unless that's what I intend to do."

Joy's heart ached. "I'm so sorry, Simon. I know what happened with your mother was horrible but that's no reason—"

Simon looked down at the papers on his desk. "We have work to do."

Joy walked into her alcove and sat down at her desk. At least she hadn't been fired for her comments. Turning on her computer, she then opened the file she needed. If Simon wanted to keep himself distant from people, even people who could help, then so be it. Her only goal was to keep this job and save as much money as possible before it ended.

She glanced back toward the office. She wished she could dismiss him easily, but something about Simon kept tugging at her emotions. She wanted to ease his resentment, show him that people were good, that they did care. But it wasn't going to be easy.

And she was a fool for even wanting to try.

Simon shut down his computer and left the office. Joy had quit work early to take Mikey to a dentist appointment. It had been a relief having her gone. With her in the alcove, he'd been unable to keep his focus. He kept reliving her comments from the other day, and each time they scratched his emotions with more force. Had she really thought he was so vain that he'd let his scar turn him into a hermit? On the other hand, was his background an equally feeble excuse?

He stood and glanced out the window, not surprised to see Mikey in the yard. How he envied his childhood. No worries, no cares. Only a pure joy in life, which he'd inherited from his mother. Joy walked across the lawn with an armful of rope. Mikey smiled and held up a plastic swing seat. Simon watched as she uncoiled the rope and attempted to fling it over the tree branch. It fell to the ground. He could see her mentally trying to figure out her next move. It was clear that if Mikey was going to get a swing today, his mom would need a little help.

He was stepping through the back door when he questioned his impulse. After their disagreement the other day, Joy may not want his help. But this wasn't about Joy. This was for Mikey. He strolled toward them, enjoying the picture they made. "Could you use a little help?"

They both spun to face him. Mikey smiled and hurried toward him, then took his hand.

"Hi, Mr. Simon. Mommy is going to make me a swing."

Simon met Joy's gaze, braced for a look of irritation, but he saw only gratitude in her pretty eyes. Maybe her irritation earlier had dissipated.

She smiled and shrugged. "I didn't think this through. Any suggestions?"

Encouraged, he reached over and took the rope. "This will do fine but we need a few more things to get it hung."

Mikey came to his side. "Here's the seat. It's green."

Simon examined the molded plastic seat. An old-fashioned wooden one would have been his preference. "This is perfect. Good and strong."

Mikey smiled and bent his arm upward. "I'm strong. I have muscles."

"Good, because you'll have to help me."

Mikey nodded happily.

Joy met Simon's gaze. "Thank you for this. He's been wanting a swing since we moved in."

Simon glanced up at the limb. He'd need a ladder and a few tools. "This shouldn't take long." He walked toward the garage.

"Where you going, Mr. Simon? Can I come?"

Joy took her son's arm. "No, sweetie. You stay here with me."

Simon faced the child. "I'm going to get some tools and things from the garage. You can come if your mom says it's okay." He watched the indecision play across Joy's face, gauging whether she should keep him at her side or allow him to venture into the strange world inside the garage.

"Fine, but be careful and don't touch anything and don't climb on anything."

Simon stifled a smile. "Would you like to come along?"

She shook her head. "No. That's okay."

"I won't let anything happen to him."

He took Mikey's hand and opened the garage door. He gathered up the things he needed and let Mikey carry the smaller items. Hoisting the ladder, he made his way back to the tree with Mikey.

"I'm helping Mr. Simon."

"I see that. Is there anything I can do?"

Simon leaned the ladder against the tree trunk. "Hold the ladder."

Within twenty minutes, Simon had the ropes secured to the branch, the seat attached and was adjusting the height for Mikey. The boy sat in the swing and pushed back with his feet to set it in motion.

"Look, Mommy, I'm going fast."

Simon glanced at Joy, surprised to see a glint in her eye. Was she crying? "Are you okay? I can take it back down if you're worried."

"No. It's wonderful. Thank you. It was very kind of you considering the things I said to you. I'm truly sorry about that."

"Don't be. There was a lot of food for thought in what you said. Sometimes it's hard to hear the truth." He held her gaze. "I hope you'll always be honest with me."

"All right." She bit her lip. "We were going to get chicken nuggets for supper. Care to tag along?"

"Sure. But do you think you can get your son out of his swing?"

She smiled up at him, sending his heart into an erratic rhythm. "That might be a task too big for anyone right now."

Their gazes locked. A sense of lightness filtered through his system. Looking into her eyes increased his pulse rate. He became keenly aware of her as a woman. A very desirable woman. He'd always acknowledged her attractiveness, but this feeling went beyond that. She was more beautiful inside than out. A woman of compassion, of devotion and generous love.

His gaze drifted to the soft curve of her mouth. She was so close that if he shifted only a few inches, she would be in his arms. He wanted her there, close to his heart. He lifted his gaze to her eyes and saw anticipation that matched his own. She blinked and stepped back and he realized what he'd been about to do.

Simon inhaled sharply. "I, uh, better get these tools picked up and put away."

"Push me, Mommy."

Joy moved quickly behind the swing and gave her son a firm push, eliciting happy giggles. Simon gathered up his tools and strode toward the garage, the boy's laughter lingering in his ears. Inside the dimly lit space, Simon set his hands on his hips and took a calming breath. What had he been thinking? He'd almost kissed Joy. That would have been a huge mistake. She was his employee. There were rules about that sort of thing and lines he shouldn't cross. He'd wondered what it would be like to kiss her, but he'd never allowed himself to dwell on that thought. But in that moment, it had consumed him and he'd almost acted. It would have been a bad choice. Besides, he needed to protect his heart and steer clear of any emotional involvement. He couldn't ever risk his heart a second time.

Chapter Five

Simon was in the process of shutting down his computer a few days later when Joy approached his desk. The apprehension in her blue eyes grabbed his attention. The workday was over. She'd left nearly an hour ago. "Is everything all right?"

Joy took a deep breath. "That depends on what you say."

"About what?"

"I have a committee meeting this evening and they usually provide childcare, but there isn't any tonight. I'm an officer, so I have to be there and so does Willa, so…" She bit her lower lip and clasped her hands together. She looked like a little girl who had asked for a special treat. "Would you be able to stay with Mikey for a couple hours? He won't be any trouble. I'll have him bathed and in his pajamas. All you have to do is put him to bed at seven thirty. He always goes right to sleep, so basically you'll just be there in case something happens."

"Like what?"

She shrugged. "Fire, burglars, tornados. You'd just be there to make sure he's safe. I'll come home as soon as I can."

Was she serious? He knew nothing about taking care of a small child. "You have no other options?"

Her shoulders sagged. "No. I didn't want to ask you but this meeting is important. It's about the bridge."

He could have guessed that much. Saving that bridge was Joy's primary concern, aside from her son, of course. Simon's impulse was to refuse Joy's request. This was way out of his comfort zone. However, he couldn't ignore the look of hope on her pretty face.

"Please, Simon. Mikey likes you. He'll feel safe with you there."

His resistance began to fade. She'd been a huge help to him in all respects. A couple hours of his time seemed a small favor in return. "What time do you want me?"

The huge smile on Joy's face and the light sparkling in her blue eyes wiped away any doubts he might have had.

"A little before seven. Thank you."

Before he realized it, he was standing at the apartment door waiting for Joy to answer his knock. She opened it with that warm smile that never failed to cause a blip in his pulse.

"Right on time."

"Hi, Mr. Simon." Mikey looked up at him with a big smile. "You want to see my room?"

Joy put her hand on her son's head. "We talked about this. You play by yourself for a while or watch TV, but you leave Mr. Simon alone. He's not like Willa—he's not here to play with you. He's here to watch over you while I'm gone. You'll be in bed soon. Do you understand?"

"Yes, ma'am. But he'll see my room when he puts me to bed. Shouldn't he see it first, so he doesn't get lost?"

Simon choked back the chuckle in his throat. "He has a point."

Joy scowled and shook her head. "I'll let you two work that out."

After a quick rundown of emergency numbers and other details, she kissed her son goodbye. "Thank you, Simon. I really appreciate this. If you need me, I'll have my phone with me at all times."

Simon glanced at Mikey, who was seated in the middle of the floor watching TV. The thought of being responsible for the child sent a chill through his veins. Why had he agreed to this? He was totally ill-equipped to care for a little boy. Mikey suddenly looked up at him and smiled, wiping his concerns away.

The moment the door closed behind Joy, Simon's insecurities flared up again. Thankfully, Mikey guided him every step of the way through a room tour, bedtime snack selection and a quick rundown of his favorite things to do. When Simon finally tucked the boy into bed, his emotions had shifted. Mikey smiled up at him from under the covers, creating a warm tingling around his heart.

"Are you going to sing me a sleep song?"

"What?"

"Mommy always sings to me before I go to sleep."

Simon shifted his weight, totally uncomfortable with the request. "I don't sing."

"Oh. Never ever?"

The question forced him to think back. He used to

sing in church. He used to sing along with the radio when he was driving. His mother sang a lot. He wasn't sure when he'd stopped. No, he remembered. He hadn't sung since the accident. "You'd better go to sleep, Mikey. Your mom won't be happy with us if you're still awake when she gets home. Maybe she can sing two songs tomorrow night."

"Okay." He smiled again. "I'm glad you're here, Mr. Simon."

When he settled into the living room, the silence began to close in on him. Normally, he liked the quiet but it didn't seem to suit this place. His gaze traveled around the cozy room. He'd only been inside the apartment for brief periods of time before tonight. He found it surprisingly efficient and homey. It reminded him of the house he'd grown up in. His mother had somehow managed to keep their small home neat and clean and welcoming. It was only when his father walked in the door that the atmosphere changed.

He doubted that would happen here. Joy's mood never changed. She was always smiling, always happy. Movement pulled his attention to his side. Mikey was coming toward him, a stuffed tiger in his arms and his cheeks wet with tears. Without asking, he climbed up into Simon's lap and rested his head on his chest. "I had a bad dream."

Simon instinctively wrapped his arms around the child, surprised at how warm he was. He smelled like shampoo and little boy. "That's too bad. But it's over now."

Mikey nodded his little head, pressing harder

against Simon's chest. "You won't let the monster get me, will you?"

"No. I won't. You're safe now." Simon realized he would like to always keep this little one safe.

Mikey tugged the stuffed toy close, and before Simon could take a deep breath, the boy was sound asleep. Now what did he do? Did he risk waking him and carry him to bed, or did he let him sleep? A quick glance at the mantel clock indicated Joy would be home soon. He might as well let the little guy sleep. Besides, the feel of the little body in his arms wasn't unpleasant. It was strangely soothing. Simon's gaze landed on the tiny hand, the thumb of which was hooked in his shirt pocket. He may be a little boy, but he had more courage than most grown men he knew.

For a few moments he allowed himself to think it was his son he was holding, that he was a father at last. How could Mikey's father walk away from him? How could he not want to stay close and protect him? If his own son had lived, even with a physical or mental disability, he would never have turned his back.

Joy stepped through the door, her eyes widening in concern. "Is he all right? Did something happen?" She hurried toward them.

Simon quickly calmed her fears. "He had a nightmare. I was afraid to move him."

Joy came toward him, arms outstretched. "I'll put him to bed."

Simon shook his head. For some reason he wasn't ready to let go of the child. He carried him into the bedroom and laid him down. Joy stepped in front of him and pulled the covers over her son and kissed him gently. Simon took one last look at the sleeping child, envying his peaceful rest.

Joy was standing in the middle of the living room when he returned, her arms crossed and her expression stern. Something wasn't right.

"Thank you for watching Mikey."

Her tone didn't sound thankful. "How did the meeting go?" Too late he realized his mistake. He had a strong suspicion how it had gone.

Joy's eyes darkened to a storming blue gray. "That was a lousy thing to do, Simon. Asking a price for the bridge land that was so outrageous no one could afford to buy it, let alone a small town like Blessing. I couldn't believe you'd do such a thing. Do you really hate this town so much or is it all about the money for you?"

There was no point in denying what he'd done. He'd asked a price nearly triple what the land was worth, hoping to end the topic once and for all. He'd done it in a moment of anger which he now regretted. He shouldn't have insulted the town council that way. He had to find a way to make amends. "I'm sorry, Joy. I was—"

She set her jaw. "You were thinking of what you want and what will make you happy. Never mind what others might want or what's more important in the long run. Maybe if you stepped out of your cave and took a look around, you'd see that there are other things of value in Blessing that have nothing to do with making a dollar." She huffed out a breath. "Typical male behavior. Do what you want then you run off leaving destruction behind."

Simon suspected she was talking about something else entirely now, but in her present mood he didn't dare ask. In fact it was probably wise to say as little as possible. "I'll see you in the morning."

Joy turned her back and he walked out into the hall, closing the door behind him. His heart and conscience were heavy on his mind as he went upstairs to his room. Somehow he'd managed to turn a pleasant evening into an obstacle without much effort. Tomorrow he'd better start working on a solution. One that would put him back in Joy's good graces.

Simon approached Joy's desk cautiously the next afternoon. They'd barely spoken today and he hadn't realized how much they interacted until it had stopped. She hadn't hummed one tune all day, which meant she was still furious with him for his outrageous offer to the city. He'd already instructed Ray to adjust the price and he wanted to let Joy know.

He cleared his throat but she refused to look up. "Yes?"

"I've lowered the asking price for the bridge land."

"I know. The mayor called me. It's still too high but we're going to try raising the amount with bake sales and maybe a GoFundMe account."

Simon knew they could never raise enough to meet his price. The thought should have pleased him. The land was his, after all, and he was under no legal obligation to sell to Blessing. His conscience flared. Morally, however, was a different matter.

Joy suddenly stood and gathered up her belongings, shut down the computer and strutted past him. "Good evening, Mr. Baker."

Simon had a feeling that digging himself out of this hole was going to take more than a price reduction.

Joy pulled into the parking lot behind the Palace Theater after dropping Mikey off at the childcare service offered by the church and parked beside Willa's car. She'd been looking forward to the meeting with the group all day. The theater had been closed a long time, but a few years ago Florence Lawson, a high school teacher, had persuaded old Oscar to rent the facility to the town and they would be responsible for the upkeep. Florence had also written a play depicting key moments in Blessing's history. They'd been hard at work for the last few months planning every detail of the performance. Tonight they would be discussing scenery.

Joy slowed her steps as she drew near the back entrance. For some reason everyone was gathered at the door. Willa met her as she approached.

"Please tell me you know what's going on?"

Joy pressed through to the door, surprised to see a legal notice attached to it stating that the theater was closed until further notice. Stunned, Joy shook her head. "I don't know anything about this. Who would close us down and why?"

Florence came forward. "We have permission to use the theater. What are we going to do? We have to work on the scenery and sets for the play. Time is running out."

Barney Hopkins, the props volunteer, looked over her shoulder. "They can't just shut us out, can they?"

Joy's chest tightened. What was happening to her town? First the bridge was threatened and now the local theater was sealed off. Her gaze went to the notice again, searching for some explanation. The name of the management firm tripped a memory and sparked her anger. She'd run across it several times at work. Squaring her shoulders, she spun around. "I'll take care of it. Y'all go home. We'll try and meet tomorrow night."

"Joy, do you know who did this?" Willa hurried along beside her as she walked to her car.

"Yes." She started the car and pulled away. And someone was going to get a big piece of her mind first thing in the morning. She refused to let Simon Baker's resentment hurt the town she loved.

Joy walked purposefully across the old wood floors the next morning, filled with righteous indignation. Overnight, her irritation toward Simon had swelled to full-blown anger. She understood Simon had his issues with Blessing, but that didn't give him the right to interfere with everything the town held dear. If he hated the place so much, he could go home.

She marched into his office, stopped in front of his desk, slammed the notice down, then set her hands on her hips, prepared for battle. "Is this your doing?"

Simon glanced up from his desk. "I don't know anything about this."

Joy huffed out a skeptical breath. "Oh really? I happen to know Pine Mark Management is connected to your inheritance. I've seen the name on several documents. What do you have against the theater? Are you deliberately trying to dismantle Blessing one building at a time?"

Simon's eyes widened. Apparently he was surprised

at her fury. He lifted the paper and tossed it down again. "I had nothing to do with this. I didn't close the theater."

"Then who did? We need access. We had work to do last night and we couldn't because of that order." She crossed her arms over her chest and took a deep breath. "We're working on the play for the bicentennial celebration and we have a lot to do before we open."

"I thought the place was empty."

Joy huffed out a surprised noise. "We got permission from Oscar over a year ago to use it, which you would know if you bothered to look into the things you own instead of slapping a for-sale sign on everything." Joy blinked away the moisture in her eyes. She would not cry in front of this man.

Simon stood and came from behind his desk. "I don't know what happened but I'll fix it. Ray was terminating our contract with Pine Mark. It was probably a misunderstanding. I promise I'll call him and straighten it out."

Some of the starch went out of her emotions. She'd expected him to mount a defense. She shifted her weight. "Good. Because we need to get back in there tonight. We have work to do."

"I understand." He came toward her. "I'm not trying to dismantle this town. I just want to sell what I own and move on."

Joy held his gaze a long moment, surprised to see sincerity in his dark eyes. "Have you seen the buildings you own? Other than the McCray building, have you been inside any of them?"

Simon shook his head and leaned against his desk. "No reason to."

Joy swallowed the snippy remark on the tip of her tongue. "There's a very good reason. Connection."

"I don't want to connect."

"You can't live your life alone, Simon. Even the most shy of us need friends and social interaction. Otherwise we simply shrivel up and die."

Simon reached over and picked up his phone. "I'll get Ray onto the theater problem. You'll be back inside ASAP."

Joy didn't bother to say thank-you. She'd save that for when the situation was resolved. She turned and went into her office with mixed emotions. Thankfully, the whole theater debacle was a mistake and Simon would make it right. However, his insistence on staying isolated from the people of Blessing was troubling.

A short while later, an email from Ray arrived explaining about the miscommunication between him and the management company. Sheila had posted the notice as a precaution, concerned that if the theater was in use it would make it harder to sell. Ray assured Joy the theater would be available this evening.

She ventured into Simon's office and stopped at his desk. "I wanted to make sure you saw the email Ray sent about the theater."

"Yes. I did."

Joy turned to go.

"Joy, I'm glad it's all cleared up. Contrary to what you believe, I'm not out to wipe Blessing off the map."

She slowly turned around as an idea formed in her mind. "Then prove it. Come to the theater with me tonight. See what all the fuss is about and meet the people who make up a part of Blessing."

Simon shook his head. "I don't think so."

Joy's irritation exploded. The man was the most bull-headed person she'd ever met. Not to mention short-sighted and self-absorbed. "You know, no one cares about your scar or your background. In fact, you'd be surprised how little other people think about you at all."

She pivoted and walked out into the hallway and didn't stop until she was inside her apartment. Maybe she wasn't cut out to be a psychologist after all if she couldn't keep her cool when someone was being a hard-headed jerk.

Mentally, she rolled her eyes. Or maybe it was just Simon who pushed all her buttons.

She had to stop trying to figure him out. The theater was open again. She'd be content with that and forget about Simon Baker.

It had rained all afternoon, but by the time Simon started for the Palace Theater, it had stopped, leaving the streets wet and the air damp. He wasn't completely sure why he'd decided to come tonight. He didn't want anything to do with a small theater group. But he did want to show Joy that he was willing to meet her half-way.

He began to rethink his decision the moment he saw all the cars in the back lot. The thought of being around all those locals, people who might remember him or his family, left a knot in his chest. However, Joy was also inside that old theater and he knew he wanted to see her and observe how she fit into this thespian world.

He spotted her the moment he stepped through the door. She was talking with a small group of women near the stage, laughing and gesturing and making the others smile. He wondered again where her sunny optimism came from. She turned and saw him, causing the others to look his way. He took a step back and gestured toward the house seats. She smiled and nodded.

Seated in the back row of the theater, he watched the activity around the stage with interest. Joy was as enthusiastic with the theater activity as she was with her job. Watching the good-natured camaraderie made him appreciate her even more. Joy Duncan gave herself fully to whatever task she chose to take on.

How did she find the energy? How did she manage to care about so many things and so many people? All he cared about was getting out of Blessing and starting his business. In a way, he envied her. She had friends all over town. Mikey's comment about needing friends came to mind. The child was right, but it took energy to make friends. It took commitment and time. He hadn't cared about anything in a long time.

Simon shifted uncomfortably in his seat, beginning to regret coming. He'd felt obligated to make amends for the mix-up last night. He'd wait a few more minutes, then slip out. He glanced up and saw a man coming up the aisle toward him. He looked for an escape but there was none. He was trapped. The only way out of a conversation would be to rudely push past. Joy wouldn't be happy about that.

"Hello, Simon. It's been a long time."

Simon stood, searching his memory for the man's name. There was something familiar about him but he couldn't place the face. The man extended his hand and Simon took it.

"I can see the confusion on your face. Phil Mason. Better known as Duke."

Simon let the handshake fall away. Duke Mason had been the bane of his existence. Always taunting him and spurring him into a fight. He'd been the cause of most of the trouble Simon had gotten into. Mason had pushed him to the point of anger and when Simon retaliated, he was the one who got in trouble. Not Duke.

The man smiled, a wide, warm and understanding smile. "I see the tumblers have fallen into place."

"You're still in town." This was the reason he didn't like connecting. Too many bad memories flying at him.

"Back in town, actually. I left, went to school then seminary. It's Reverend Mason now. I returned about seven years ago to pastor the Peace Chapel church. I hear you're now the proud owner of the Afton Grove estate."

Simon was still trying to process meeting his nemesis. "Not proud. Just the owner but hopefully not for long."

Duke chuckled. "Not what you expected, right?"

Someone called for Pastor Phil and Duke met his gaze. "We'll catch up soon, Si. I have a lot of apologizing to do and a big load of forgiveness to seek." He smiled then walked away. Simon watched him go, trying to reconcile the boy who had made his life miserable as a teen with the man of the cloth he'd become.

How could someone like Duke change so drastically? More to the point, if he could change, maybe Simon could, too.

But where did he start?

Chapter Six

Joy found her focus torn between the activity of the theater group and keeping an eye on Simon, who had sequestered himself in the back row of theater seats, as far away from people as possible. She shouldn't be surprised. He'd come tonight to appease her, but her hope for getting him involved with the locals would be a failure if he persisted in keeping to himself.

Forcing Simon from her mind, she gave her full attention to the night's agenda. The next time she glanced up at Simon, she noticed Pastor Phil walking up the aisle toward the back row. Even from this distance, she could see the expression on Simon's face. It was the same one she'd seen the day Viola Doyle had spoken to him. Not good.

She hurried across the theater and up the wide aisle, hoping to reach Simon quickly. Her concern grew when she saw Simon's shoulders brace and his chin lift. She quickened her steps. The last thing she needed was an incident the first time she convinced her boss to step out in public. By the time she made her way to the back of the theater, Phil was gone and Simon had walked out into the lobby.

She hurried through the double doors and found him seated on the steps leading to the balcony. His hands were clasped and his head bowed. At least he hadn't left. She approached slowly, searching for a starting point. Easing herself down beside him, she waited for him to say something. When he remained silent, she decided to speak up.

"Is everything all right? Did Pastor Phil say something to upset you?"

Simon huffed out a breath. "Pastor. What a joke."

"What do you mean?" What did he have against the reverend?

"Duke Mason was the biggest bully in town. No one was safe from his torment. Especially me."

Joy tried to wrap her mind around the image Simon was painting. Phil Mason was one of the godliest men she'd ever known. Lacking words, she gently placed her hand on Simon's forearm in a gesture of comfort, only it had a different effect entirely. She became aware of the warmth of him, the strength beneath his tanned skin. She pulled her gaze away from his arm and looked into his eyes. Her heart skipped a beat. He looked away and inhaled a breath.

"It's hard to believe he was like that."

"Well, he was. Now he's a man of God."

Simon said the words as if they were a bad thing. "What did he say to you?"

"He wants to talk about forgiveness and apologies. As if that changes anything."

"It can. It can change you both. I'm sorry I talked you

into coming. I just wanted you to get out and see something other than those two rooms you live in. Maybe you're right. There are too many bad memories here in Blessing. I guess I don't understand because all mine are so good."

Simon rubbed his palms together as if contemplating something. She waited for him to speak.

"Not all of them are bad."

He faced her and she saw a softness in his dark eyes she hadn't seen before. She touched his arm again, hoping to encourage him to continue.

He glanced around the large lobby. "This place was my refuge. I could come here and hide from all the stuff at home and the pitying, disapproving looks from people. Sitting in the dark, losing myself in a movie, was like spreading wings and flying above all the pain and frustration of my life."

Joy's heart warmed and she gently squeezed his arm. "Is that why you became a pilot? So you soar above all the sadness?"

He shrugged. "Maybe. It's the only place I feel completely free, completely myself."

"I'm glad you found a safe place to come back to, then."

Simon captured her gaze, as if searching for understanding. He looked away again before continuing. "Mr. Hall owned the theater back then. He hired me to sweep up after the movies and fill the candy counter. I wasn't very dependable. I could only come when my dad was out of the house. He didn't like Hall. I never understood why, but my dad didn't like me working for him. My erratic work schedule never bothered Mr. Hall. He welcomed me whenever I would show up and in return he let me use the theater whenever I needed to. He let me sleep here a few times."

"He sounds like a wonderful man. What happened to him? Is he still here in town?"

"I don't know. I haven't thought about him in years. Not until tonight."

"Maybe you should look him up. Let him know how important he was to you."

Simon shook his head. "No point. He wouldn't remember me."

"Pastor Phil did. People like to know they've made a difference in someone's life."

Simon abruptly stood. "I need to leave. I have some things to take care of."

"Yes, of course. I'm sorry I asked you to come, Simon."

He walked to the front door then glanced back. "Don't be sorry. I'm glad I came."

She smiled and nodded. "Good." She watched him disappear through the wide front entrance, puzzled by his behavior. Had she said something wrong? Or had she touched another sore spot with her boss? She could never judge his reaction to things. There were so many layers to Simon Baker, she doubted she'd ever understand him.

Maybe she wasn't supposed to.

Lightning and thunder took over the night sky, accompanied by strong gusts of wind, as Simon drove home. He barely noticed. He was too busy kicking himself for going to the theater in the first place and then for not staying and waiting for Joy to finish. Instead, he'd behaved exactly the way Joy had observed. He chose to run and hide.

Inside his office he sought the comfort of his easy chair, his mind replaying the evening's events. Two encounters, each so different, had skewed his perceptions. Phil Mason a minister. The boy who had terrorized Wilson Junior High was now a benevolent man of God. How was that possible?

He laid his head on the back of the chair. He'd been caught off guard by the memories of Mr. Hall and working at the theater. It had been his safe place, his only escape. He'd even toyed with the idea of becoming an actor so he could live in the cocoon of the theater forever. Mr. Hall had been like a father to him. Maybe he should look him up and let him know how important his help had been. Joy had a better grasp of those things than he did. As much as he hated to admit it, Ray was right. Joy was proving to be a blessing in his life in ways he'd never expected.

She was forcing him to take a closer look at his choices and decisions. His hermit-like existence wasn't protecting him. It was trapping him, chipping away at his identity until he didn't know who he was anymore. He couldn't go on this way.

He was about to go upstairs when a noise from the other room drew him up from his chair. He walked out into the hall and looked around, then stepped into the front parlor. When his eyes adjusted to the dim light, he saw Joy standing at the large front window. Her posture hinted at a melancholy mood. The lightning and thunder still raged outside. Was she afraid of storms?

He approached quietly, not wanting to alarm her. "Joy." She moved her head but didn't turn to face him. "Are you all right?"

"Yes."

Her voice was soft as a whisper. He moved closer. Too close. He caught a whiff of her flowery perfume. Or was it the shampoo in her hair? She always smelled like spring. He pushed those observations aside. "What are you doing here?"

She faced him then. "I'm just watching the rain and the lightning. God's power and grace on display. I'm sorry. Am I intruding?"

"No, of course not. But it's late. I expected you to be with Mikey this time of night."

"He's spending the night with Willa. They're having a campout."

"I thought she lived in an apartment."

Joy laughed softly. "She does. They put up blankets in the living room and eat hot dogs sitting on the floor. Willa tells him scary stories and they sing songs. They both love it."

"Willa sounds like a grandmother type."

"She is. I'm glad he has that in his life. I adored my grandmother."

"I never knew either of mine."

Joy's eyes filled with compassion. He wanted to look away but he couldn't.

"I'm sorry I made you come to the theater tonight. I should have respected your position and let it be. But I truly believe that avoiding the things you fear only gives them more power."

"It was my choice. But I have to ask why you're so determined to get me out into the community."

"I don't like seeing you in pain and so angry at the world."

"Why?" He held his breath, braced for her answer.

"Because I care about you. We're friends—at least I hope so."

Her statement sent a warm flow around his heart. "We are." He realized that he wished it was more. Much more.

She smiled. "Good. We all need friends. Even loners like you. I think I understand now why you keep yourself separated from the people here. Each time we've gone into town, you've been assaulted by painful reminders of the past."

She lifted her hand and for a moment he expected her to touch his cheek. But she lowered it and turned to look out the window again. "I love watching the rain. It makes me feel safe and warm."

"Isn't that backward? People are normally afraid of storms."

She laughed softly. "I've never been accused of being normal. My mother always told me I was a Pollyanna and sooner or later my cheery outlook would come up against the harsh realities of life. She was right."

Simon resisted the urge to brush a stray strand of hair from her forehead. "But you're still a very optimistic person."

She smiled over her shoulder at him. "I'm also known for being obstinate."

"I like you obstinate. I like you cheerful. I didn't realize that my life was missing sunshine until you came along."

She looked into his eyes and the air between them sparked like the lightning outside the window. She was the most fascinating, beautiful woman he'd ever known. He could easily see her as part of his future. But he couldn't do that to Holly. He'd loved his wife too much. Joy held his gaze a moment then stepped back.

"Good night, Simon."

She walked away, leaving him with a cool chill on his skin and an uncomfortable knot in his chest. His feelings for Joy were growing and he had to find a way to stop them. Holly was the only woman he would ever love. There was no room for anyone else.

Saturday arrived with sunny skies and pleasant temperatures, a perfect day for a little boy to be outside. Joy closed the door on the dishwasher, pushed Start, then headed outside. Her gaze sought out her little boy, finding him perched in the limbs of a small tree near the pergola. Her heart flooded with fear and she opened her mouth to shout for him to get down. With only one strong hand, climbing a tree was dangerous. Mikey looked at her and waved and she readjusted her thinking. She'd vowed to give her son the freedom to explore and test his limits.

Swallowing her concern, she walked toward him. He looked happy and triumphant. She stopped and looked up at him. "So, how did you get up there?"

"I just climbed."

She nodded. "And how about getting down?"

His expression turned to puzzlement. "I don't know."

Joy set her hands on her hips, inwardly full of pride at her son's courage. "Then you're in a pickle, aren't you?" Mikey began to study the tree, gauging each branch and the distance to the ground. He was only three feet up in the air—not much chance of him getting seriously hurt. Still, Joy's heart tightened with concern. She watched as he stretched out his leg, feeling for the lower branch. He gripped a smaller limb with his three fingers, his good hand wrapped firmly around the thicker limb. She always marveled at the strength in those three little fingers.

She held her breath as Mikey slowly made his way lower then let go and dropped to the ground.

He raised his arms over his head with a huge smile. "Ta-da."

She opened her arms and he ran to her. "Good job, sweetheart." She turned around and froze. Simon was standing a few yards away, doubled over, his hands on his knees. Was he ill? Had he been hurt? "Simon?"

Slowly he straightened, his expression one of extreme relief. Mikey ran toward him.

"Did you see me? Did you see me climb that huge tree? It was awesome."

Simon nodded. "I did. You were like a cat up there." He met her gaze over Mikey's head and Joy saw the fear and relief in his eyes. He'd been afraid for her son.

Mikey gave Simon a high five then ran to his swing. Joy made her way toward her boss, who still looked a bit green around the gills. "Are you okay?"

He exhaled a quick breath. "I am now. I came out and saw him up in that tree and I thought…"

Joy smiled. "Me, too. My heart stopped when I saw

him. But I couldn't take away his sense of adventure and his pride of accomplishment."

Simon held her gaze. "How do you do that? I would have snatched him out of the tree so fast—"

"And then he would feel like he'd failed and that you didn't trust him to take care of himself. Then the next time he wanted to try something new, he'd be fearful and insecure."

"You're amazing."

"Hardly. I just want Mikey to grow up like a normal kid. Not someone who needs special attention."

A big smile spread across Simon's face and Joy's theory was finally confirmed. His smile was devastating. His dark eyes twinkled, his firm mouth lifted at the corners revealing strong white teeth and charming laugh lines at the corners. Her heart warmed, then dissolved into warm syrup seeping all the way down to her toes. Simon Baker was a very handsome man. She'd suspected his smile would be a stunner but the real thing left her weak-kneed and breathless.

When she found her voice, her brain wasn't fully operating. "Oh, Simon. You should do that more often."

"What's that?"

"Smile." Her cheeks warmed. She'd said the word in a hushed and dreamy tone like a teenage girl with a crush on the new boy.

He held her gaze, his dark eyes boring into her. "I'll make sure I do if you enjoy it so much."

Tension vibrated between them, as if there were an invisible cord slowly drawing them together. Her simple appreciation for Simon's good looks had transformed into full-blown attraction that had her wondering what it would be like to kiss him. Without thinking, she raised her hand, wanting to touch him, to be physically connected.

"Mommy! Mr. Simon! Help."

She and Simon turned as one and ran toward the pergola. Mikey waved them forward.

"Hurry. He's hurt. Real bad."

Joy reached him first. "Who's hurt?

Mikey pointed to the corner of the pergola. A soft whimper came from the thick trunk of the vine that covered the wooden structure. Joy took a step forward only to find Simon's hand on her arm.

"Let me look." He pulled the leaves aside then hunkered down. "It's a little dog. He looks injured."

Mikey lunged forward. Simon wrapped his arm around his torso to hold him back. "He's hurt. Let's not touch him. He might bite."

Mikey pouted. "But he needs someone. Can we keep him? I'll help him get better."

Joy pulled Mikey away.

Simon looked up at Joy. "Can you get me a pair of gloves from the garage?"

With his hands protected from sharp teeth, Simon gently stroked the frightened animal. The dog whimpered again and yelped when Simon touched his paw. "He looks like he's either been in a fight or maybe gotten his paw stuck in something." Simon gently lifted the injured pup and cradled him against his chest.

Mikey started to cry. "Mommy, he's hurt."

Simon spoke softly to the boy. "It's okay, Mikey. I'll take him to a puppy doctor who'll make him all better."

"Can I pet him?"

Simon exchanged looks with her. She nodded. "If you think it's safe."

Simon stooped down. "He's scared, Mikey, so be very slow and gentle."

Mikey lifted his left hand, using his thumb and forefinger to pet the dog's head. "It's okay, doggy. Mr. Simon will fix you like he fixed my swing."

Simon stood and looked at Joy. "Do you know a good vet?"

"Yes. Leann Watkins. Her clinic is on Jenkins Street off Church Street."

Simon started toward his truck.

"Mr. Simon, wait." Mikey raced after Simon. "You'll bring him home won't you? He needs me."

Simon met her gaze. "I'll try, buddy, but the doctor may have to keep him for a while to make him better."

"Okay." Mikey reached up and touched the little dog. "Be good, Pickles. I'll wait here for you."

Joy rested her arm across Mikey's shoulders. "Pickles?"

Mikey nodded and looked up at her with sincere eyes. "He's in a pickle like I was when I was in the tree."

Her heart swelled with love. "That's a perfect name for him, then."

Simon knocked on the apartment door a few hours later, a knot of anxiety churning in his chest. He had no idea how Joy and Mikey would take the news about the dog. His tension was reflected in Joy's blue eyes when she opened the door. She motioned him in, biting her lip in anticipation. "How's Pickles?"

Simon couldn't help but grin at the name. "He's

going to be okay, but—" Joy groaned and placed her fingers over her mouth.

"How bad?" She sat on the sofa looking up at him, seeking reassurance.

He sat down beside her, resisting the urge to take her hand. "Dr. Watkins said she'll probably have to remove part of his paw, but that he'll be fine in the long run."

Mikey ran into the room and stopped in front of him. "Where's Pickles?"

He drew the little boy close. "He's still at the dog hospital. Dr. Watkins is taking care of him."

"When can he come home?"

"Not sure yet, buddy. We'll have to wait and see how quickly he gets better."

Joy pulled the boy into her lap. "Could she tell what happened to the poor little thing?"

Simon shook his head. "She did say he was probably a stray. He was underweight and in need of care."

"Can I keep him when he's all better?"

Joy smoothed his hair. "Oh, sweetie, I don't know. This isn't our house, remember?"

"It's fine with me, speaking as your landlord."

Mikey smiled and lunged into Simon's arms. "Thank you. I'll take good care of him. He'll be my best friend. Can we go get him and bring him home tomorrow?"

Joy smiled at her son. "Not yet, sweetheart. Pickles is still hurting and the doctor has to have time to fix him up. His paw was hurt very badly and she might have to…remove part of it."

Simon held his breath for the boy's reaction. Mikey looked between him and his mother. "Will he have a boo-boo like me and Mr. Simon?"

"Maybe."

Mikey smiled. "See, he needs me. I'm going to go pray for him." He slid off the couch and dashed into his room before slamming the door.

Simon absently touched his cheek, his gaze on Joy's face. "He takes after you."

"Oh?"

"He forms attachments quickly." Joy met his gaze a long moment and he thought he read an admission in the blue depths. Did she have an attachment to him? He hoped so.

"He has a tender heart." She looked away briefly. "Thank you for letting him keep the dog. He's been asking for one for a long time. Did Dr. Watkins say when Pickles could come home?"

"Not for several days. I'll keep in touch and let you know." He stood. Being in the small apartment, so close to Joy, was making him anxious. Being near her always made him restless and edgy. Her proximity played havoc with his pulse.

She followed him to the door. "Please let me know how much the bill is."

"I'll take care of that. After all, the pup was found on my property, so it's my responsibility." The smile of gratitude she gave him made whatever the cost worthwhile.

He turned away but Joy called him back. "Simon, we're having a birthday party for Willa tomorrow afternoon. Why don't you join us?"

For a brief moment he considered accepting, but then he thought of facing a bunch of people he didn't know and shook his head. "I wouldn't want to intrude."

"You wouldn't be. It's just close friends. Arlo and his gram will be here and Willa and us. I promise you'll feel comfortable."

His resistance melted with her kind words. She never failed to think of others no matter what the situation. "All right." The smile she gave him sent his pulse racing and a warm rush through his system.

"Good. See you at two o'clock."

Simon already regretted accepting the invitation. He didn't do parties, especially with strangers. He had a feeling it was going to be a long wait until tomorrow.

Chapter Seven

Joy checked the clock again. Dinner was almost ready and everyone was here except Simon. She'd reminded him at church this morning, but she wouldn't be surprised if he failed to show up. Disappointed, but not surprised.

The knock on the door came as Willa was placing the first piece of catfish into the skillet.

Joy opened the door with a smile. "I was afraid you wouldn't come."

Simon lifted an eyebrow. "Did it matter so much?"

Her cheeks warmed. It did but she wasn't sure why. "Yes. Of course. You're…our friend."

"I'm afraid I came empty-handed. I had no idea what to bring."

She shook her head and closed the door. "You brought yourself—that's all that's important." She glanced away. Her tone had conveyed more than she'd intended. She was surprisingly delighted to have him here. In the kitchen, she gestured to the round table in the corner of the kitchen. "I think you know everyone." She sensed Simon stiffen and remembered that he'd not met Arlo's grandmother. "Miss Millie, this is Simon Baker,"

Millie smiled and stretched out her hand. "I remember you. Your mama adored you. She'd be proud of you, son."

Joy watched the play of emotions over Simon's face, but wasn't quite sure how to read his reaction. Thankfully, his mood lightened as they enjoyed the meal. Willa had prepared the catfish to perfection, as well as the hush puppies. The vegetables were fresh and tasty and the coleslaw a tangy complement. Conversation was light and amusing, and Mikey kept them all entertained with stories about finding Pickles.

Simon smiled at Mikey. "I saw Dr. Watkins at church this morning and she said Pickles might come home in a few days. He's doing very well."

Mikey grinned from ear to ear. "Will he live with me?"

Simon nodded. "If you want him to. And if you'll take good care of him."

"I will. I promise. Mommy, we have to get a bed and bowls and toys and stuff."

Joy chuckled and ruffled his hair. "Let's get him home first."

"Can he sleep with me in my bed? He'll feel safer that way and he won't have any bad dreams."

Joy exchanged a knowing smile with Simon. "We'll talk about that later."

Arlo scooted back from the table. "I need to go, Gram. Me and the guys have plans."

"What kind of plans?"

He shrugged. "Just plans."

Millie pursed her lips together and motioned for her grandson to sit down. "Well, your friends will have to wait until we're finished with our meal. It's not polite to leave before dessert."

Arlo lowered his voice and leaned toward his grandmother. "But it's important. I need to be there."

Millie aimed a stern scowl at her grandson. "Have you forgotten you have to drive me home? There's nothing so important that a few teenage boys can't wait for half an hour."

Arlo slumped in his chair, arms crossed over his chest, clearly upset.

Joy noticed Simon studying the boy a moment then he glanced at her. She had the feeling he was trying to convey something.

"How's the theater group coming along, Joy?"

Joy took a sip of her drink, trying to follow Simon's lead. "Great. Of course, we can always use more help." Simon cast his gaze at Arlo then back to her. She had an inkling of where he was going. "Simon, how are you with a hammer?"

"I can swing one pretty well. My brother-in-law was a contractor. He taught me the basics."

"Great. We need help building the sets." She smiled at Arlo. "How about you? We could use a strong young fella to handle those two-by-fours."

The teen frowned and shrugged. "I'm not into that artsy stuff."

Joy frowned. "That's too bad. We have several high school girls in the group but not many guys. And we'll need people to be in the play and help with the behind-the-scenes stuff."

Arlo frowned. "When is it?"

"Thursday nights. I think the girls were going to bring a few more of their friends this week."

Arlo looked at Simon. "Will you be there?"

Joy tried not to giggle at the look on Simon's face.

"Uh, yeah. Sure. I was there the other night."

Arlo glanced back and forth between her and Simon. "I don't know much about building."

"Not a problem." She took a bite of her hush puppy. "You and Simon can be a team. He'll teach you everything he knows."

Simon gave her a sardonic glance. "I'd be happy to be your instructor."

Joy grinned and patted Simon's shoulder. "This will be fun. All of us working together to make the bicentennial play the best it can be."

From the doubtful looks Joy received from Arlo and Willa, she knew she'd have to be both cheerleader and referee in this arrangement to keep everyone on track.

Conversation over dessert centered on the upcoming monthly events leading up to the official bicentennial weekend next spring. This month was a hot-air balloon fest, and a decorating contest was scheduled for next month. Local clubs and organizations would take a downtown lamppost and festoon it with harvest decor.

Mikey finished his pie then looked at Arlo. "Want to come and kick the ball with me?"

Arlo shrugged. "Sure." Millie touched his arm as he passed. "I'll be done shortly then we can leave." Arlo muttered a "Yes, ma'am" then followed Mikey out the back door.

Simon leaned toward Joy and spoke softly. "Thanks for picking up on my idea for Arlo."

"What brought that on?"

"I saw him hanging with that same group of boys after church today. I don't think they're the kind that will do him any good."

"You could tell by looking?"

Simon nodded. "Let's just say I recognize the type."

Joy took a bite of the Mississippi Mud Pie Millie had brought. "I like the idea of him helping at the theater. That was a good call."

"It was until you dragged me into it."

She looked over at him, relieved to see a twinkle in his brown eyes. "It'll do you good, too."

Millie smiled over at him. "Simon, if you don't mind me asking, how did you injure yourself?"

Joy froze. She sensed Simon brace. His jaw was flexing and his mouth was in a tight line. Her heart went out to him. It had been a really enjoyable afternoon until now. She should have anticipated this and spoken to Millie before Simon arrived. Under the table, she laid her hand lightly on Simon's leg, offering emotional support.

Slowly, he lowered his fork to the plate, taking time to answer. She prayed he wouldn't say something he'd regret. When he finally spoke, his voice was thick with pain and she longed to hold his hand, but he had them fisted on either side of his dish.

"It was a car accident three years ago in Charlotte, North Carolina."

Simon kept his gaze lowered and spoke through clenched teeth.

"It happened during a freak winter storm. High winds. Heavy snow. They called it the Speedway Blizzard. A teenage driver ran through the intersection at full speed and hit us head-on. My wife and child were killed. I got off with only a…scratch."

"I'm sorry, son." Millie leaned forward, reaching a hand out to Simon. "I lost my daughter, Arlo's mother, in a car accident. I know how painful it can be."

Joy barely heard Millie's words. The room faded into a blur and her breathing increased. Her mind was locked into a dark cave, struggling to grasp what Simon had said. His accident had happened during the Speedway Blizzard. So had hers.

The latent, unexplainable fear mushroomed in her head again. What did it mean? Why did she keep having these frightening feelings and snippets of recollection where Simon was concerned? Why did they give her this sick dread in the pit of her stomach? The first pangs of a migraine shot up into her skull. She rubbed her temple in a futile attempt to forestall it but the pressure began to build.

"Joy. Are you all right?"

Simon's voice floated into her mind from far away. She was vaguely aware of him touching her arm, but the pain in her head was increasing. She pushed away from the table, her legs shaky. "I, uh, I'm sorry but I'm getting one of my headaches. Excuse me."

Joy made her way to her bedroom on sheer instinct. Her vision was blurred with pain and confusion. Closing the door, she then sank onto the bed, too upset to even take her pills.

What was happening to her? Could the fear be another symptom of her post-concussion syndrome? The doctors had said she could suffer long-term effects for the rest of her life.

Tears stung her eyes. *Please, Lord. Help me find the answers.* These feelings were terrifying.

Simon started to go after Joy but Willa spoke up. "She'll be fine. These things sometimes hit without warning. She suffered a severe concussion in her accident and it left her susceptible to these fierce headaches." She patted his arm. "Let's let her rest."

Simon nodded in agreement even though his protective instincts made him want to go to her and offer comfort. Instead, he helped clean up from the meal, played a game with Mikey and worried. Willa checked on Joy but said she was resting and encouraged him to leave, assuring him that Joy would be fine in the morning.

Back in his office, Simon paced, unable to shake Joy's reaction. He was tempted to go back to the apartment and check on her, but Willa's car was still in the drive, so he knew she was in good hands.

He went over the conversation before she'd hurried out. He'd been telling Millie about his accident, but Joy knew all about that. What could have upset her? Willa's explanation did little to ease his concern, but at this point he had no choice but to trust her judgment.

Lowering himself into his easy chair, he thought back on the afternoon meal. He'd been surprisingly comfortable sitting at the table with her friends. It had been a long time since he'd felt as if he belonged anywhere.

Until Miss Millie had asked about his scar.

His first impulse had been to leave, but then he'd felt Joy's hand on his leg and knew she was encouraging him to face his pain. It hadn't been as hard as he'd expected. Perhaps Joy and Ray were right. He couldn't keep living alone with the anger and bitterness. Somehow, Joy had made looking at the past a little easier.

He had to face the fact that Joy and Mikey were becoming more and more important to him. He looked forward to bringing the dog home and seeing the happiness on the little guy's face. Making the child happy, seeing Joy happy, was like stepping into a bright light after being in the dark.

Worry over Joy's reaction pushed other thoughts aside. He remembered a few times she'd suffered these headaches, but she'd never left work. There was something different about this one that left him deeply troubled. Unfortunately, there was little he could do until morning.

In the meantime, he doubted he'd get much sleep tonight.

Joy looked up as Willa entered her bedroom. She'd managed to swallow her meds and then fallen asleep. "What time is it? How's Mikey?"

"Eight in the evening and he's playing in his room. Are you feeling better?"

Joy did a quick mental inventory. "I think so. The headache is gone." Willa's expression reflected her cu-

Get up to 4
FREE FABULOUS BOOKS
You Love!

To thank you for being a loyal reader we'd like to send you up to 4 FREE BOOKS, absolutely free.

Just write "YES" on the Loyal Reader Voucher and we'll send you up to 4 Free Books and Free Mystery Gifts, altogether worth over $20, as a way of saying thank you for being a loyal reader.

Try **Love Inspired® Romance Larger-Print** books and fall in love with inspirational romances that take you on an uplifting journey of faith, forgiveness and hope.

Try **Love Inspired® Suspense Larger-Print** books where courage and optimism unite in stories of faith and love in the face of danger.

Or **TRY BOTH!**

We are so glad you love the books as much as we do and can't wait to send you great new books.

So don't miss out, return your Loyal Reader Voucher Today!

Pam Powers

LOYAL READER
FREE BOOKS VOUCHER

YES! I Love Reading, please send me up to 4 FREE BOOKS and Free Mystery Gifts from the series I select.

Just write in "YES" on the dotted line below then return this card today and we'll send your free books & gifts asap!

➡ — YES — ⬅

Which do you prefer?

☐ **Love Inspired®** Romance Larger-Print 122/322 IDL GRJD	☐ **Love Inspired®** Suspense Larger-Print 107/307 IDL GRJD	☐ **BOTH** 122/322 & 107/307 IDL GRJP

FIRST NAME

LAST NAME

ADDRESS

APT.#

CITY

STATE/PROV.

ZIP/POSTAL CODE

EMAIL ☐ Please check this box if you would like to receive newsletters and promotional emails from Harlequin Enterprises ULC and its affiliates. You can unsubscribe anytime.

LI/SLI-520-LR21

riosity and concern. "I'm sorry I left like that. I couldn't think straight."

"I don't remember you having a headache this bad before." She sat on the edge of the bed.

"I haven't." Joy raked her hair from her face, searching for the right words to explain.

"Do you remember when I mentioned that Simon's name sounded familiar and I told you he lived in Charlotte? He said his accident happened during the Speedway Blizzard." She swallowed. "So did mine."

Willa frowned. "I don't understand. Why should that matter?"

"I don't know. But ever since I met Simon, there's this gnawing in my mind, like when you see someone from your past but you can't quite recall the name. Only this is dark and ominous, like the leftover pieces of a bad dream."

"Maybe that's all it is and you're reading too much into it."

"Maybe, but I keep having these quick flashes like scenes from a movie. I remembered seeing Simon's full name on a piece of paper, and the other night I woke up thinking there was a policeman standing at my bed. It doesn't make any sense." She took her cousin's hand. "I wish Grandma Nell was still alive. She was with me through everything. She could give me the answers."

"I know. But didn't the doctors say your memory might come back in pieces and that they might not make sense?"

Joy nodded and brushed her hair off her face. "But there's something different about this. I can't explain it. I just know that I get a sick feeling in my stomach when I think about the accident."

"Well, if you ask me, I think it's time you called your doctor back in Charlotte. Tell him what's going on and see what he has to say. I'll bet this has nothing to do with Simon at all. It's just time for your memories to start coming back and he just happens to be your focus right now."

It was the first sensible thing Joy had heard. Maybe Willa was right. Her odd impressions and the nagging anxiety were all jumbled up with her new life working for Simon and she did have a lot of frustration in their relationship. She nodded. "That's a good idea. I'll call him tomorrow." Could it be that simple? She doubted it. "But don't you find it curious that we both had serious accidents at the same time?"

"Not really. Charlotte is a big city, and that storm affected hundreds of people, not just you. You're letting your imagination run away with you."

Joy kept her gaze on her hands. Willa was right. Her missing memory had always worried her.

Willa started to leave then stopped. "Joy, do you have feelings for Simon?"

The question caught her by surprise. "What? Of course not. He's my boss. I mean, we're friends, good friends, but that's all. There are no romantic feelings between us." Joy stared at the tissue in her hands. That wasn't entirely true. She couldn't deny that she found Simon attractive. It was something she'd puzzled over because he wasn't her type at all. He was too stern, too reclusive, too self-absorbed.

"Are you sure? I hear a note of affection in your voice whenever you speak of him."

Joy shook her head. "That's sympathy you hear. Nothing more. I understand his loss and I know how hard it is to dig out of that kind of grief. Chad might not have died, but my world was left just as empty when he walked out."

"Okay. If you say so." Willa gave her a hug. "I'm going to take Mikey home with me so you can rest. I'll take him to school in the morning and then come by and check on you."

Joy spent a restless night and woke in the morning groggy and anxious. Her dreams had been an assortment of scary scenes of streets and flashes of light and visions of Simon looming in the shadows. The headache had eased but still lingered. There was no way she could work today. No way she could face Simon yet. She sent him a text explaining then fixed a cup of coffee. She was on her third cup when Willa knocked at the door. "Are you feeling any better?"

"How's Mikey?"

"He sends a hug. I made him pancakes for breakfast. He asked about you a lot." Willa joined her at the kitchen table. "By the looks of you, the headache is still holding on."

Joy nodded. "I told Simon I wouldn't be in this morning."

Willa leaned forward. "I did a little research last night. Would you like to know what I found?" Willa pulled out a paper from her purse. "The Speedway Blizzard caused a seventy-five-car pileup on the interstate and over five hundred accidents. Everything from fender benders to fatal wrecks. A dozen people lost their lives." She laid the paper down. "Your accident was only one of hundreds during that storm."

Joy smiled at her cousin and held her hand. Willa always made her feel better. "I spoke with Dr. Collins a while ago and he said what I'm experiencing isn't unusual. Everyone regains their memory differently. Some never get it back. He said confusing fragments of memory can often become tangled up with current stresses."

Willa spread her hands wide. "There, you see. Nothing to worry about."

Joy mulled over her cousin's comments the rest of the morning and by late afternoon she had accepted the fact that she was making a mountain out of a molehill with her odd recollections. Determined to put the fear behind her, she dressed and prepared to report for work.

Keeping busy was the best way to deal with this situation. Dwelling on it had accomplished nothing. Besides, she never liked missing work.

Simon debated checking on Joy most of the next morning to see if she was better but decided to let it rest. However, when Dr. Watkins called with news of Pickles, he had the perfect reason to go to the apartment.

His nerves were on edge as he waited for her to answer his knock. Was she feeling better? Hopefully, his report on the dog would lift her spirits.

"Simon. Good morning."

He took a quick inventory of his tenant. She looked better this afternoon. Rested and more like her normal self. He was relieved to see that bright light in her eyes again. "I wanted to see how you were doing."

"Much better, thank you. I apologize for yesterday. When these headaches hit, all I can do is lie down until they go away."

"No need to apologize, though I need to. I never thanked you for the wonderful meal. It's been a long time since I had a home-cooked meal with friends." She smiled and his pulse skipped.

"I'm glad. Willa makes the best catfish in town. When her diner reopens, you'll have to make a point to stop in."

There was a challenge in her smile that he knew he'd accept as soon as possible. "I will." He held her gaze, losing himself in her blue eyes. "I have another reason for stopping by. The vet said Pickles can come home today. He'll need some special attention for a week or so but he's recovering nicely."

"That's wonderful. Mikey will be so happy. I guess I'll have to take him to the pet store when he gets home."

Her smile warmed him through to his toes. "No need. I've already picked up everything you'll need. All you have to do is supply the love."

"Thank you. That's very generous. I'm sure Mikey will give Pickles all the love he needs and more."

"I have no doubt. Every boy should have a dog."

She cocked her head and her eyes warmed with a sweet smile. "Did you?"

"For a while. My dad chased it off."

"I'm sorry. We'll be happy to share Pickles with you. After all, he'll be living on your property."

The teasing in her tone made him smile. "That's very

generous." He stepped back. "I'll be back with Pickles within the hour."

"We'll be waiting. Oh, and, Simon, I'll be at work tomorrow."

"Good. The office feels empty without you."

Simon couldn't keep from smiling as he drove into Blessing a few minutes later. He looked forward to seeing Mikey's face when Pickles came home.

When he knocked on the apartment door later, his nerves were again on edge, though not from worry but from excitement over Mikey's reaction. He didn't have long to wait. Mikey pulled open the door, his eyes wide and a huge smile on his face.

"Pickles. You're home." Joy hurried in from the other room. "Welcome home, Pickles."

Simon set the dog crate down near the fireplace.

Mikey sat on the floor, gripping the bars. "Can I get him out? He looks like he needs a hug."

Simon stooped down beside the cage. "Let's let him get used to things first." He looked at Joy. "I have some meds for him to take, but Dr. Watkins says he should be okay to treat normally. The bandages on his paw can come off next week."

"What's wrong with his foot?" Mikey looked up at him with a worried expression.

"Remember I told you his paw was badly hurt? They had to operate and take off one of his toes." Simon braced for the boy's response.

Mikey spread his arms across the front of the cage. "It's okay, Pickles. I know what to do for you. I have things missing, too."

Mikey abruptly stood and threw his arms around Simon's neck. "Thank you, Mr. Simon, for saving my dog. Pickles and I will love you forever and ever."

Simon nearly choked on the lump in his throat. The little arms around his neck squeezed tightly. He enfolded the little boy in his arms, enjoying the warmth and the affection. "You're welcome, Mikey." An overpowering swell of love flooded his heart. This might not be his son, but the sensation was no less powerful. It was the sweetest feeling he'd ever known.

One he would gladly enjoy every day for the rest of his life.

Chapter Eight

Joy glanced up as Simon came into her alcove a few days later. Life had settled back into a normal pattern though with a more warm and friendly atmosphere. Simon had changed. The scowl was gone from his rugged features, his shoulders were relaxed and he actually smiled now and then. She couldn't explain it but if she had to guess, it had something to do with Mikey and Pickles and his daily check-in on their relationship. Simon had helped out at the theater last night and started teaching Arlo basic carpentry skills. He'd fit in well with the others. She attributed it to the fond memories he had of the Palace as a place of refuge.

She smiled and held up her hand. "Before you ask, yes, Pickles was a good boy last night. He didn't whine once. I think he's getting used to being in the cage overnight."

He chuckled softly. "Still not letting him sleep with Mikey."

"Nope. That's not going to happen."

Simon shook his head. "You are a very mean mother. Mikey told me so."

"I know. He tells me that every day." Simon smiled and her heart did its now-familiar flip-flop. His phone rang and he walked back into his office, leaving her with a funny buoyancy inside her rib cage that made it difficult to focus on her work.

She'd barely gotten started when she heard someone enter Simon's office. She recognized Sheila Dixon's voice. Curious, she rose and went toward his desk.

Sheila turned and smiled. "Hi, Joy. You'll want to hear this. I come bearing good news."

She sat down and pulled a folder from her briefcase. "I have an offer on the theater." She handed the file to Simon. "Do you know Hank Robinson?"

Simon frowned but Joy spoke up. "I do. He owns several large car dealerships in the state."

Sheila nodded. "Robinson Chevrolet. Five dealerships across the South. Well, it turns out he has a passion for restoring old movie theaters and he wants yours, and he's willing to pay a pretty sum."

The huge smile on Simon's face sent Joy's hopes plummeting into her toes.

Simon nodded. "I know that name. Isn't he the guy who revived that old jingle about seeing the USA in your Chevrolet?"

Sheila crossed her arms in triumph. "That's the one."

Simon studied the paper. "This changes everything. With the theater sold, that leaves only the estate and the hotel. I can finally get back to Charlotte and get my business up and running."

Joy tried to calm her fears. "Sheila, what will Robinson do with the theater? Will we still be able to use it? You know we have events scheduled through the bicentennial."

Sheila grinned. "No worries. He knows all about that. He plans on sprucing up the place for the 200th birthday, then after that he'll do a full restoration and leave it in the hands of a local manager."

Joy breathed a small sigh of relief. At least he wasn't going to take over and shut out the locals. But her mood quickly deflated when she realized that the sale meant Simon would be leaving Blessing.

The realization that she might not see Simon ever again hit like a blow to her chest. She didn't want to think about him not being in Blessing. She would miss him. He'd become a good friend and she enjoyed working for him. She cared about him more than she should.

She slipped back into her alcove as Sheila and Simon discussed the details of the purchase agreement. She stood at the window, looking out on the lush yard. If Simon left, she'd be out of work again. And homeless. It was all over. The job, the home, the extra money. The diner and the apartment wouldn't be ready for several more weeks, which meant they'd have to move in with Willa again. And what about Pickles?

Joy turned from the window, arms crossed over her chest. How would she tell Mikey that Simon was leaving? He'd be heartbroken. He'd grown very attached to her boss. And what would happen to the rest of Simon's inheritance? He still had the old hotel and the estate to dispose of and, of course, the bridge. Would he settle that issue now that he had what he'd come for? She had to get an answer from him before he left.

The lease was up soon and the town's GoFundMe account wasn't growing. All the money the city had was going into the upcoming events. Without the bridge, the Blessing bicentennial would be a diluted celebration.

Joy set her jaw and squared her shoulders. There wasn't time now to try to persuade Simon to do the right thing. She'd have to confront him head-on and make him see the importance of the situation before he left town.

Sinking into her desk chair, she toyed with a paper clip as her thoughts swirled. Despite her determination, she'd started to lose her heart to Simon. Day by day she discovered a deeper layer to the man, a warmer, softer core that he kept protected with a shell of anger and bitterness. She doubted if he fully understood what he was doing. She'd promised herself she'd help him shed the grief and allow himself to feel joy and happiness again.

And, maybe, love.

She was a fool. All she could do now was devote her time to saving the bridge.

Nothing else mattered.

By the time Simon finished going over the details of the theater sale with Sheila, Joy had gone home for the day. He'd been so focused he hadn't noticed her leave. He wanted to celebrate. After all this time, things were finally starting to come together. Sheila had told him she'd also received nibbles on the old hotel. He could be free of this inheritance in a matter of weeks. He'd been impressed with Sheila's abilities and felt confident in leaving the sale of the remaining properties in her hands. He could start packing today and concentrate on his new business.

Glancing out the window, he caught sight of Pickles scampering across the lawn, Mikey following behind. His throat tightened. Leaving Blessing meant leaving behind Mikey and Joy. The thought shouldn't have impacted him so strongly. Somewhere along the way, he'd developed feelings for them both. Mikey had stolen his heart from the beginning. Joy had been a slower, more subtle attachment.

Simon rubbed his forehead. He'd been fighting the attraction for Joy for a while now and was seriously concerned that he might be falling in love with her. He couldn't let that happen. He could never risk his heart like that again.

A knock on the doorframe pulled him around. Ray came into the room with a huge smile on his face. "I had to come and congratulate you on the good news about the theater sale." He extended his hand and Simon grasped it briefly.

"Yeah, it was great. Out of the blue."

Ray lowered himself into a chair. "You don't sound as happy as I expected. Within the last few weeks, you've sold half of your inheritance and at well over your asking price."

Simon nodded. "Enough money so I can go back home and get my charter service underway." Ray studied him a moment and Simon braced for one of his lectures. It had to be the lawyer in him that couldn't help but give advice.

Ray clasped his hands together and stared. "If I had

to guess, I'd say you're having second thoughts about leaving Blessing."

Simon shook his head. "No. I won't be sorry to leave this place behind."

"What about the people? Like maybe Joy and Mikey?"

Simon set his jaw. "I don't know what you're talking about."

Ray shook his head in disbelief. "Are you really that out of touch with your emotions that you can't see you're in love with those two? And from what I've seen, they're pretty fond of you, too."

"You're wrong."

Ray shrugged and stood. "If you say so. But I don't think leaving Blessing will be as easy as you think."

Ray's observation lay like a stone in Simon's chest. He couldn't deny it and he couldn't acknowledge it. He ran a hand down the back of his neck. Returning to this town had complicated his life more than he'd ever anticipated.

Everything had been so clear when he'd arrived. Sell and get out. Now everything was murky and confusing. Despite his best efforts, he'd allowed part of himself to get attached to this place and two very special people.

Now he had to find a way to disengage. Quickly.

Simon jogged onto the porch that afternoon, not bothering to do his cool-down stretches. For the first time in a long while, his run hadn't cleared his mind or settled his irritation. He needed a place to go and escape the emotional silt that was continually stirred up from being in this town. Ray's remarks about his feelings for Joy had only made it worse.

A short while later, he pulled his truck to a stop at the county airfield, where his private plane was parked. There was only one place where he could find peace and solitude. Being in the air allowed him to unshackle his mind from the past and his grief and breathe. He focused his attention on his preflight check then climbed into the cockpit and prepared to take off.

When he was surrounded by clouds and vibrant blue, his heart rate slowed, the fog in his head drifted away, and there was only him, the controls and God's sky. He let his thoughts float like the clouds around him. They settled upon Joy and Mikey. The thought of leaving them hit him harder than he'd expected.

Simon turned the yoke to the right and flew over downtown Blessing. He'd intended to fly over farmland, but he'd ended up viewing the town from above. The old courthouse looked much smaller from this height. The four streets around the central park looked charming and picturesque. This must be the appeal Joy saw. From this vantage point, he could almost agree with her, but once he landed, he'd see the truth again—a small town filled with small minds and hearts of stone.

Joy's passionate words replayed in his mind. *Blessing is a wonderful place to live.*

He had to admit when Joy was beside him, the town didn't seem so bad. She had a way of brightening everything around her. Mikey, too. He found himself eagerly looking forward to seeing the little guy each day. Mikey had settled permanently into his heart and there was no getting him out. He was afraid Joy might be doing that, too.

Simon made another pass over Blessing, lower this

time, noticing the people on the sidewalk, the cars coming and going and the activity on the riverbank path. All together it did paint a very picturesque image of the town. He was forced to see the town with different eyes. That was Joy's influence. He wasn't sure he liked that.

Banking, he headed back to the airport, promising himself to invite Joy up with him the next time. She'd enjoy getting a bird's-eye view of her beloved Blessing. He would enjoy having her beside him to share the freedom and exhilaration he experienced when he flew.

Truth was, there were many things he'd like to share with Joy.

Joy inhaled a deep breath. It was time to fish or cut bait, as her grandma used to say. The lease on the bridge land was quickly approaching and Simon had no reason to stay in Blessing now that the theater was being purchased. There was no way she'd let him leave town without making a decision on the land. Normally, she would wait for the most opportune time to plead her case, but knowing Simon's distaste for this town, he was probably already packed and had a taxi waiting to take him to the airport.

Her nerves were quivering as she made her way to the office, but she refused to let anxiety stop her from forcing a decision. The town's 200th birthday was too important to too many people. She prayed Simon's attitude had softened with the good news of the sale and he'd finally listen to reason.

She stepped into the office and huffed out a breath. Empty. Simon was always here. It was late afternoon. Where could he be?

"You looking for me?"

Joy gasped and turned around. "Don't scare me like that."

"Didn't mean to." He walked past her and sat at his desk. She took a moment to collect herself then approached. "We need to talk."

Simon inhaled a slow breath. "A woman wanting to talk is never a good thing."

"Neither is a man avoiding decisions."

Simon worked his jaw. "Let me guess. The bridge."

"Yes. Now that you'll be...leaving, something has to be decided."

"Why?"

"Are you serious? A million reasons. The town, the people, the tradition, symbolism. Oh, and that little thing called a bicentennial. The lease is almost up. We need to know what you're going to do."

"I don't know. Like I said, it's not at the top of my to-do list."

"It should be. You have your money, so why don't you just donate the land and be done with it and help the town?"

"And why would I do that? The town never cared about me or my family when I was growing up here. Why should I care about the town?"

A flurry of emotions swirled up through her chest. Anger, hurt, disappointment all clogged her throat, and tears formed behind her eyes. "That's not true. Mr. Hall cared." She set her jaw. "I thought you'd changed. I thought you'd come to see that not everything you remember about Blessing was the way you believed. I thought since you got what you came for, the money and getting rid of your inheritance, you'd at least find it in your heart to grant this one small request to the city."

Simon looked away, his fingers rubbing his chin in a gesture she'd come to understand meant he was getting upset. She swallowed and plunged ahead. "Why do you hate the bridge so much?"

"I just think it's time people stopped worshipping it, that's all."

"Worshipping? No one does that."

"Really? They come and pray thinking their prayers are going to be answered, that whatever they want will be granted. Just because some woman back in the fifties prayed on the bridge for her polio-afflicted son and he got better. They might as well toss coins into a wishing well. People are too gullible. It's time they moved on."

Suddenly Joy understood. "Your prayers weren't answered." A look of surprise flashed through Simon's eyes. She'd hit her mark. Sensing he might need to vent, she sat down and waited.

He was silent a long while before answering. "I went to that bridge every day asking for God to heal my mom. To make my dad stop drinking. For someone to help. I never got an answer."

The pain in his voice tore at her heart. She could see a young Simon desperate for help and not getting the answers he'd prayed for. "I know how that feels. I prayed for things that I didn't get. But I do believe prayers are answered. Though not always in the way we would like." Her heart filled with compassion. "Sometimes God says yes. Other times he says no or not yet. Our prayers tend to be selfish ones. God knows what's down the road and maybe he's preparing us for something that's to come."

"And what was he preparing me for when he allowed my mother to die so young?"

The bite in his words hit like a physical blow. "I don't know. What was he preparing me for when he allowed my husband to abandon me and Mikey?" Joy searched for something encouraging to say. "Didn't you tell me that going to live with your sister and her husband had turned your life around? Maybe God knew you would need help to face the next part of your life."

Simon held her gaze, his dark eyes probing. "I don't have any answers, Simon. But I know that bridge offers comfort and solace to a lot of people. It's a place to come and reflect, no matter what their troubles, their beliefs or their level of faith. It's worth preserving."

"You're too optimistic."

"You're too pessimistic." She had to make one last try. "What if you allowed access to the bridge just until the celebration is over next autumn? Then you can sell it or tear it down or whatever your black mood dictates at the time." She stood and started to go then turned back. "You said people here need to move on. Well, so do you. You're not the only person on the planet who's lost a loved one or didn't get the life they expected, but I didn't have the luxury of hiding inside a dark hole and condemning the world. I had a son to take care of. I had to make a living and I had to deal with my loss and move on."

Simon refused to respond or even look at her. "I thought you were starting to come out of your cave but I guess I was wrong. It's so much easier to blame everyone else. That way you don't have to take responsibility or deal with the grief. Well, as far as I'm concerned, you can just wallow in it for the rest of your life."

Tears streamed down her cheeks as she hurried away. She hadn't meant to be so harsh but the man was infuriating.

And the bridge was too important.

Simon stood at his bedroom window staring out into the fading light. From here he had a view through the trees to the Blessing Bridge. When the home was built, it would have looked out onto the lush well-kept gardens of Afton Grove. He'd run across a picture while going through Oscar's records. The bridge wasn't the only structure in the garden. There was a small Greek Revival structure called the Sanctuary tucked into the back corner near the edge of the pond where the cypress knees poked through the shallow water. Closer to the old mansion, a small gazebo overlooked the pond from the sloping lawn. The old photos had also shown a large fountain in the middle of the pond. The gardens would have been spectacular in their day. He couldn't blame the city council for wanting to return the one surrounding the bridge to its former glory.

As he watched, a woman walked across the bridge. Joy? No. This woman was tall and slender, not petite like Joy. His heart hardened as he watched the woman stop in the middle of the bridge. What was she praying for? Did she realize she was wasting her time?

Joy's words pricked his conscience. She'd hit her target and he couldn't ignore the truth any longer. He slipped his hands into his pockets. He knew why he hated the Blessing Bridge. It taunted him. If he went there and prayed, the Lord would demand he forgive and he wasn't about to do that.

He turned from the window, Joy's accusations filling his mind. She was wrong. If God wouldn't answer the prayers of a devout believer then he wouldn't answer anyone's. But he couldn't avoid this decision on the bridge much longer. He didn't want to leave Blessing with bad feelings between them. But he wasn't ready to forgive, either. He probably would never be. But he could keep a promise and help out at the theater.

Thursday evening, Simon entered the theater through the back door, Arlo right behind. Joy came toward them smiling, though Simon could see it lacked her usual wattage. Her anger at him hadn't completely subsided.

"I'm glad you could make it. There's a lot of work to do. I hope you brought your tool belts." She turned and called out, "George. Your helpers are here."

Simon knew by the tone of her voice and her body language she was still unhappy with him. He wanted to grant her wish but he couldn't. All he could do was try to make it up to her somehow.

A slender gray-haired man came toward him, hand outstretched. "George Russell. Thanks for coming to help."

Joy walked away briskly, further cementing Simon's status as being in the doghouse. George quickly outlined what he needed done then left Simon and Arlo to assemble the pieces of scenery and props. Simon enjoyed instructing Arlo on using the power drill and nail gun. The kid was a quick learner. Getting him involved in the theater had been a good idea.

"So how did you learn about tools and building and stuff, Mr. Simon?"

"My brother-in-law. He taught me enough that I could earn my way through college working in construction."

"Is that what you do, build stuff?"

"No. I'm a retired Air Force pilot."

Arlo lowered the power drill and studied him. "You mean you flew fighter jets?"

Simon grinned. Everyone thought that if you were a pilot in the service you were a top gun pilot. "No. That's a Navy flyer. I flew a radar plane."

Arlo mulled that over a moment. "How did you learn to do that?"

"The Air Force taught me."

"I think it would be cool to fly a plane."

"There's nothing like it."

Arlo raised the drill and set the next screw. "It probably costs lots of money for lessons."

Simon nodded. "It's not cheap, unless you join the service, then it's free."

With the first task complete, Simon went in search of George while Arlo went to talk with the girls from his school. George grinned when he approached.

"You don't remember me, do you?"

Simon searched his memory but found nothing to identify the man. "Sorry, I guess not."

"Your mom worked for me for years. The best employee I ever had."

The cylinders clicked into place. "Mr. Russell. Russell Furniture. Yes, sir, I do remember you. My mom loved working for you."

"And we loved her. We were devastated when she got sick. We tried so many times to help out but..." He shrugged. "You know how your dad was. He made it impossible. No matter what we tried, he rejected it."

Simon tried to grasp what the man was saying. "I'm sorry, I don't understand. What did my father do?"

George looked surprised and puzzled. "He refused any help whatsoever. We sent food, but he'd return it by tossing it in our trash. We tried to add a little to her paycheck, but he'd bring it back. It wasn't only that. He'd make a scene in the store each time. It was beginning to affect our business. We finally stopped trying. All we could offer then were our prayers."

Simon's stomach knotted. "I didn't know. I had no idea."

"Maybe we should have tried harder."

"No. I'm sure my dad would have sabotaged whatever gestures you offered."

Simon was putting away the tools when Joy came toward him. Mentally he prepared an apology, but she spoke first.

"I'm sorry, Simon. I was out of line earlier. Your feelings toward the bridge are your own, and I have no right to try and impose my needs and wishes on you. Whatever the outcome, Blessing will survive, with or without the bridge."

She'd intended to make him feel better, but all her kindness did was make him feel petty and selfish. He started to respond but Arlo interrupted.

"Are we going to start on that arbor tonight?"

"Look who's all gung-ho all of a sudden." Simon grinned. "We're done for the day, get your things together." He faced Joy, who studied him a moment before smiling.

"Channeling Mr. Hall, aren't you."

"What?"

"Mr. Hall. The manager here. He helped you, so you want to help someone else. I like this side of you, Simon. You should show it more often. Thinking about others suits you."

She walked off, leaving him wondering if she'd had a double meaning to her statement and questioning his continued stance on the bridge land.

Maybe he should follow Joy's hint and think of what she wanted and what the town wanted. He was leaving. He could put the past behind him and move forward, leave the bad memories in the dust once and for all.

Unfortunately, he now had many good memories, too.

Simon dropped Arlo off at home then turned his truck toward the estate. He caught sight of the sign marking the Blessing Bridge as he passed by and for a moment he considered pulling over and paying a visit. His cell phone chimed and he glanced at the screen. His investor was calling. He drove on, then pulled to a stop at the end of his driveway to take the call.

Ten minutes later, Simon hung up, all thoughts of the bridge forgotten. His investor had pulled out. He'd found a more profitable venture, one that was already up and running. That left Simon back at square one. There was no way he could start a charter service on his own, even with the money from his inheritance. He never would have embraced the idea if he hadn't had an investor. Maybe he could still pull it off if he sold the estate and the hotel. Otherwise, he was stuck here again.

The idea didn't bother him as much as it would have before. Going back to Charlotte meant leaving Joy and Mikey behind and that thought left a big knot in his chest.

When had they become so important to him?

Chapter Nine

Simon parked his truck near the front of the house then climbed the broad steps to the front porch. His head was pounding. His life used to be so simple but now it overflowed with problems. Joy's pressure to save the bridge, dealing with old memories, the stress of trying to unload his inheritance, and now the loss of his investor was the latest blow to his plans.

Add to that the fact that Joy had started to take over more and more of his thoughts and a space in his heart. Mikey had already claimed a chunk of it. They frequently played with Pickles in the evenings and he looked forward to their time together. He'd even started to have thoughts of the future. Things he'd never believed he would want again. But the idea was impossible. His life was elsewhere.

"Hello, sonny."

Simon jerked his head toward the far end of the porch. His chest tightened and his throat collapsed. The man smiled and saluted. Heat surged up through

Simon's torso. The last person he wanted to see again was Buck Baker. His father.

Buck spread his arms wide. "Glad to see me? It's been a long time. I hardly recognized you, boy."

"What are you doing here?" He ground out the words through clenched teeth.

Buck stood and sauntered forward. "I came to see you. My boy. My only son."

Simon recoiled when his father drew near. The smell of alcohol hung around him like a wreath. "Why?"

Buck scratched his thick stubble. "It's long past time. I should have come to see you sooner but, well, I thought it was time for a family reunion."

The ingratiating smile on his father's face unleashed an explosion of anger. His father didn't know the meaning of the word *family*. "Reunion. So you invited my sister and her family to visit, too?" It was all he could do to keep the hatred out of his voice.

Buck waved a hand to one side. "Well, you know, she and I were never very close and with all those kids…"

"She has two daughters. Not exactly a houseful."

Buck smiled and nodded. "Ah, but it's not the same as the bond between a father and son, now, is it?"

Simon's stomach was churning just being around his parent. "What do you want? Why are you here?"

Buck slid his hands into the pockets of loose-fitting, ragged pants. "Well, sonny, time is passing. The years are starting to catch up to me. I'm not as spry as I used to be. I figure it's time to settle down and spend time with the ones I love."

Simon was beginning to see the picture now. His no-good father had learned about the inheritance and had come to lay claim to a portion for himself. He should have anticipated this. "You could have saved yourself a trip. There's no money here. Only a lot of old buildings for sale."

Buck glanced around. "Maybe. But once you sell out, there'll be plenty to go 'round, right, sonny?"

"No, there won't. You're not getting a penny out of me." He turned toward the door but his father grabbed his arm.

"Now, don't go getting all high-horsey. I'm your old dad. I need a place to stay for a few days while I get my bearings and rest up. I'm not getting any younger, you know."

"So you said." The touch of his father's hand on his arm made him ill. He wanted the man gone. It was typical of his selfish father to crawl out of the woodwork once he smelled a free ride in the wind.

Buck clicked his tongue. "Now, that's not very charitable of you, boy. Your mama wouldn't be happy with you."

Simon yanked his arm away then pointed a finger at his father. "You have no idea what my mother would like."

Buck's eyes narrowed. "Maybe not. But I'm still your daddy. Like it or not."

Simon hated that the man was right. He couldn't simply shove his father off the porch, as much as he wanted to. It went against his nature. He faced the older man and held his gaze. "You can stay the night. But tomorrow you're out of here. Do you understand?"

Buck smiled. "That's real kind of you, sonny. I appreciate it." He glanced up at the large house. "You may not have money but I'm sure you have a nice soft bed and a good hot meal. That's the least you can do for your own daddy, eh?"

Simon gritted his teeth. There was no use talking to the man. He'd milk any kindness to the max for his own comfort. Simon entered the house, keenly aware of his father on his heels. He strode up the stairs and opened the door to one of the guest rooms at the end of the hall. He watched his father enter the room, scanning the decor and calculating the value of each item.

"Very homey." Buck smiled, his eyes twinkling with anticipation.

Simon started to leave. He couldn't take another moment with the man.

"I'm looking forward to a hearty meal later."

Simon turned his back, speaking without looking at his father. "It's late. If you're hungry you can fix yourself a sandwich." He strode off down the stairs, fighting to control the anger pounding in his chest. From the time he'd been dropped off at his sister's house when he was fifteen, thoughts of his father hadn't entered his head. To him, the man was dead. Now he turned up on his doorstep with his hand out, eager to take advantage of the situation.

Simon sought refuge in his office, wishing Joy was at her desk. He needed some of her positive outlook at the moment. He couldn't find anything good in his father's sudden appearance, and he had no idea how he'd endure the man's presence. Worse yet, he didn't know how he'd keep Joy and Mikey from the man's degrading influence. Buck Baker never had a kind word for anyone.

When he saw his father pass by on his way to the

kitchen, he decided he'd better join him. No telling what he'd steal to feed his gambling habit and his need for drink. Buck had his head in the refrigerator, searching for something to eat. The sooner he fed the man, the sooner he could retreat to his room. Reaching around Buck, Simon pulled out a casserole he'd had delivered from the grocery and placed it in the microwave.

"Aw, I knew you'd do the right thing. You always did. You and your mom were always too soft for my liking."

Simon clenched his fists. "Don't talk about my mother."

Buck laughed. "See. Too soft."

Simon strode from the room.

"What's the matter, sonny? Too good to eat with your old dad?"

Simon went upstairs to his room then shut and locked the door to keep his father out. Keeping him out of his thoughts, however, was a different problem. As he stood at the window, his gaze fell on the Blessing Bridge faintly lit by moonlight. For a moment, he considered paying a visit.

Pointless. He had to get through the night, then he'd make sure his father left town first thing in the morning. He wouldn't allow him to spend any more time in his home than necessary.

After a restless night's sleep, Simon rose early the next morning. He wanted to be in the office when Joy arrived so he could warn her about his guest. Buck wasn't known for his social skills. He was more likely to spew out curse words and rude remarks, which he saw as humorous. He didn't want Joy subjected to any of that.

When Simon entered his office, his father was already there seated at Simon's desk, looking through a stack of papers. Simon clenched his teeth. "Get up. Now."

Buck grinned and lifted his hands. "Okay, okay. Don't get yourself in a knot. I was just looking things over. It's my right as your dad."

Simon pushed past his father and sat down. "You have no rights."

"We're family. What's yours is mine, so to speak."

"No. It's not."

Buck took a seat in front of the desk and leaned back. "What kind of scam did you work on old Oscar to get him to leave you his fortune?"

"No scam. I just outlived everyone else. I told you, there's no fortune, just a bunch of old buildings that no one wants."

"The old goat must have left you a tidy sum. This place ain't exactly a hovel, now, is it?"

Simon fired up his computer. "It'll be up for auction soon. No one wants it. Especially me."

Buck scowled and leaned forward. "It's our heritage. You need to honor that."

Simon nearly choked on his anger. "It's not our heritage. This is Mom's family line, not yours, and you don't know the first thing about honor."

"Good morning, Simon. I had an idea about the hotel."

Simon looked up as Joy entered the room. She stopped when she saw Buck.

"Oh. I didn't realize you were in a meeting."

Before Simon could explain, Buck jumped up and faced Joy, giving her a leering once-over.

"Well, well, this must be the lovely Mrs. Baker. You did all right, sonny. She's a real looker."

Simon quickly stood and moved around his father and went to Joy's side. She looked shocked and he didn't blame her. "I'm sorry, I'd hoped he'd be gone before you got here."

"Ha. Afraid I'll take her away from you?"

Simon moved a little closer to Joy. "This is Joy Duncan, my assistant. Joy, my father. Buck Baker."

Buck moved forward but Joy recoiled, pressing slightly against his side. "Hello."

"Assistant, huh? Is that what they're calling it these days?"

Joy gasped and looked at him for help. Simon turned his back on his father and caught Joy's gaze. "I won't be needing you today. You can report back to work tomorrow." He was relieved when he saw understanding bloom in her eyes.

"Okay. Thank you." She peeked around him and nodded toward his father. "Nice to meet you." She gave Simon a grateful and sympathetic smile and hurried off.

Buck grinned and scratched his chin. "You have good taste. She's a pretty little wife, that one."

"She's not my wife."

"Then you're more stupid than I thought."

Simon went back to his desk. "I have work to do. You need to leave."

"And go where?"

"Anywhere but here."

"Fine way to treat your old dad."

"Hey, Mr. Simon. I get to stay home today. Cousin Willa was going to watch me 'cause we don't have school, but now Mommy gets to stay home, too."

Simon hurried around his desk and went toward Mikey. He needed to get the boy away from his dad. "That sounds like a fun day. Why don't you go back to your mom and we'll play with Pickles later."

"But I wanted to see you. I missed you."

Buck came closer then gasped. "What the— What's wrong with his hand?" Buck spewed out a few blue words. "I might expect you to sire a freak of a kid."

Mikey's lip poked out and tears began to roll down his cheeks. "I'm not a freak."

Simon scooped him up and held him close as the boy buried his face in Simon's shoulder. "Shut up, Dad. What's wrong with you?"

"Nothing, but that brat of yours is deformed."

Mikey started to sob. Simon hurried from the office and down the hall to the apartment. He didn't bother knocking on the door. "Joy!"

She hurried into the room, her gaze landing on the sobbing child in his arms. "What happened? Is he all right? Mikey, what's wrong?" She reached for him but he refused to let go of Simon. "I thought he was in his room."

"My dad said something ugly to him. I'm sorry. I tried to get him away from the office, but I wasn't quick enough."

Joy gently rubbed Mikey's back, making soothing sounds. Slowly his crying eased and he released his hold on Simon's neck and turned to his mother. Joy cradled him close and sat on the sofa with him in her lap.

He looked up at his mother with tearstained cheeks and sad eyes. Simon's heart was aching.

"That mean man said I was a freak and deformed."

Joy held him closer, rocking back and forth. "Shh. He's wrong. He didn't understand."

Simon watched as Joy slowly calmed her son and then suggested he go outside and play with Pickles. He smiled and dashed off, leaving Simon to envy his ability to recover from an upsetting experience. "I'm so sorry. I never dreamed Buck would say something like that to Mikey."

"It's not your fault. And it's not the first time people have reacted that way when they see Mikey's hand. I try and teach him to not let those comments upset him, but he's just a little boy. Maybe someday he'll be strong enough to let them roll off."

A fierce sense of protectiveness swelled inside Simon. He wanted to stand with them and make sure nothing like this happened again. And he knew just where to start. He stood. "Keep away from my dad. I'll make sure he's gone by the end of the day."

Joy reached up and took his hand. "Simon, don't make trouble on our account."

"I'm your boss and your landlord. I have to watch out for you both."

Without letting her reply, he turned and headed back to his office. His dad was stretched out on the sofa at the other end of the room, watching TV. Simon grabbed the remote and pushed the power button. "Get out. You're not welcome here."

Buck slowly sat up. "I'm your father. You can't talk to me like that."

"I just did."

"Oh, I see. Old Oscar leaves you a big inheritance and now you're too good for your family."

"You're not family. Just someone I'm related to. Leave. Now." Simon sat down at his desk, resisting the urge to punch the man in the face.

Buck sneered. "You're just like your high-and-mighty uncle. I came to him when I lost my job with the plumbing company. I needed a little help and he had the nerve to offer me a minimum-wage job as if I was some snot-nosed kid. I deserved a management position."

"So you turned him down?"

Buck cut loose with a string of expletives. "I didn't need his charity. I was perfectly able to take care of my family."

Simon's anger overflowed. "But you didn't, and Mom died."

"I wasn't going to take handouts!" Buck's loud voice reverberated through the room. "People were always trying to make me look bad, bringing around food and money and flaunting their superior lives in my face." Buck leaned his hands on Simon's desk and let loose with a diatribe of the injustices he'd suffered from the people of Blessing.

Simon stood. "That's enough. Get out."

Buck didn't flinch. He straightened and shrugged. "Got nowhere to go. No means to get there if I did."

Simon reached into his pocket, pulled out his cash, grabbed his dad's hand and slapped it into his palm. "Now you do."

Buck picked through the bills then shrugged. "That

won't keep me away for long. Can't get very far on this piddling amount."

"Go. And stay away from my fam—friends."

Buck must have realized he'd pressed too far. "I'm going. Don't blow a gasket." He walked toward the door, then turned and held up the cash. "Say goodbye to that pretty wife of yours and that sickly kid, too."

"They aren't my wife and child. Mikey is Joy's son."

"So you say." He walked away laughing loudly.

Buck's hateful vibe lingered long after he'd gone, making it hard for Simon to accomplish anything. All he wanted to do was be with Joy and Mikey and make sure they were all right. He doubted Joy would want him around right now, given what his father had done.

Things Buck had said began to settle in Simon's mind. His attitude toward taking help fit with the things other people had told him. Viola Doyle and Millie had both hinted at their thwarted attempts to help his mother. George Russell, too.

Could he have been wrong about the lack of help from the people of Blessing? Had they held out a hand only to have Buck smack it away, preferring to let his family suffer to maintain his skewed sense of pride?

Joy had tried to tell him he was wrong about the residents, but he'd been so certain he was right, that his resentment was fully justified. Now he wondered if he'd had it all wrong. His dad was the culprit. Not the locals.

Thankfully, Buck didn't return that day, but Simon had a feeling his father wouldn't pass up an opportunity to sleep in the guest room again and grab a couple of free meals. Simon knew from experience that his dad wasn't easily discouraged, and right now he was convinced Simon had a golden ticket and he was fully entitled to his share.

He had to find a way to get Buck out of Blessing and convince him that there was nothing here for him to come back for.

Joy kept a close eye on Mikey the rest of the morning but he seemed his usual happy self, his encounter with Simon's father apparently forgotten. She wished she could dismiss it as easily.

Her heart ached for Simon and the life he must have endured with the likes of Buck Baker for a father. Losing his mother and his family had only pushed Simon's resentment and anger deeper into his heart. She hoped the unpleasant man would be gone soon, for all their sakes.

Concerns over Simon wore at her mind. The best way to avoid that was to bake.

After gathering up the ingredients, she called Mikey inside and started mixing up a batch of chocolate-chip cookies. Spending time with her son pushed everything else out of her mind.

Curled up on the sofa later, Joy allowed the silence to soothe her spirit. Mikey was taking a nap and she had a few glorious minutes to herself. Turning on the TV, she checked the local news channel. A police officer appeared on-screen talking about an incident in Hattiesburg.

A memory exploded in her mind, drawing a soft gasp from her throat. She closed her eyes as the images swirled around. Ben Jones. The name of the policeman standing at the foot of her hospital bed with a very serious expression. He said something but she couldn't hear him.

Pressing her hand to her temple, she willed herself to remember, trying to draw comfort from the things her doctor had told her about her returning memory. But this time it was different. This flash of recollection brought a new level of anxiety with it. Why?

Picking up her electronic tablet, she searched for information on the Speedway Blizzard. What she found supported what Willa had mentioned earlier. The storm had lasted for two days, hundreds of cars were involved in accidents and twelve people had died. If only she could remember a complete span of time. These mental snapshots only made her more confused.

Joy heard the back door open. Willa must have arrived. She'd texted she was coming by.

She entered the room and glanced down at the tablet in her lap. "What are you doing?

"Looking up the Speedway Blizzard."

Willa took a seat. "Learn anything important?"

"No. I did have a new flash of something." She explained about the officer."

"Hmm. That's strange. Nothing else?"

"The fear is stronger now."

Willa stood and went to the kitchen, returning with two glasses of sweet tea. "Let's start at the beginning. What do you remember about that night?"

"Very little." She rubbed her forehead. "I remember leaving the office. I'd planned on leaving work early, but something came up at the last minute and I had to stay. I remember snow was making it hard to see."

"Do you remember getting hit or running into anything?"

Joy buried her face in her hands. "No. I remember a flash of light, then sliding, but nothing else until I woke in the hospital. They told me I'd been unconscious for a day, and that I had a broken arm and other injuries. The day I left the hospital, a policeman came to talk to me. Ben Jones. Why would I remember his name?"

"What did he want?"

Joy dug deeper into her mind. "He said something about charges, but that's all I remember."

"Did they think you'd been responsible for the accident?"

"Maybe, but nothing ever happened. My grandmother said she got a notice that my crash was declared an accident. Case closed."

"Did you get a copy of the accident report? Maybe that would tell you something."

"I did but it was lost in the fire with my other important documents. I've applied for replacements on everything, but I didn't for the accident report. It didn't seem important at the time. Now…" She shrugged and brushed her hair from her forehead. "I don't understand why I keep having this impression that I know Simon's name. It doesn't make sense."

Willa smiled. "That's the point. It doesn't make sense but you're trying to force it to. I think you should stop worrying. After all, it's merely a string of unrelated events you're trying to connect. And—" Willa pointed a finger at her "—didn't you work at a walk-in clinic during that time? For all you know, Simon could have been a patient and that's where you saw his name."

There was a lot of sense in what Willa said. In fact, before working at the clinic, she'd worked at a bank. Their paths could have crossed there, as well. "You may be right."

"I know I am. You just concentrate on your new life and the possibilities you have ahead of you. You deserve some peace and happiness."

Joy longed to take her cousin's advice, but she couldn't stop her brain from searching for those long-hidden memories. Somehow she had to get them back and learn the truth.

She was running down a rain-slicked street in the dark. Someone was after her, but she had no idea who or why. Before her loomed a patch of black ice stretching out for miles. She had to stop or she'd slide into a bottomless pit. Her feet hit the ice and she screamed.

She woke, forcing her breathing to slow and letting her heart rate return to normal. This had to stop. She needed answers. Throwing off the covers, she then retrieved her tablet and went in search of the Charlotte police website. She clicked on the link to request an accident report. The document appeared and her heart began to palpitate. All she had to do was fill in the blanks, hit Send and then wait. She would have the answers in a matter of weeks. No more questions, no more doubts. She gulped in a quick breath. But what would she find? Would the answers ease her mind or add to her torment?

Lord, what should I do? Why am I so afraid?

She thought back to what Dr. Collins had said about letting the memories return at their own rate. Forcing them would only create more stress, and stress worked against the process. Ignoring the doctor's advice wasn't a good strategy. Neither was caving to fear, but tonight, fear was the winner.

After lying back down, Joy tugged up the covers. She'd give her spotty memory a little longer to recover. Maybe she'd be able to conquer her fear in the meantime. All she needed was a little more time.

And a big load of courage.

Chapter Ten

Simon was sorting through a new pile of papers he'd discovered in old Oscar's cabinet a few days later when Ray arrived. "What brings you by? We still on for our steak dinner tomorrow?"

"Yes, but I needed to talk to you and it's best done in person."

Alarms went off in Simon's head at the odd tone in his friend's voice. "What's happened? A problem with the estate?"

"No, not directly." Ray took a deep breath. "Your father came to see me today."

Simon exhaled an irritated breath. That was the last thing he'd expected Ray to say. "Why?"

"He wanted to know if there were any provisions in Oscar Templeton's will for other relatives, or any bequests that might have been overlooked."

Simon couldn't believe what he was hearing. Apparently, there was no end to Buck's greedy nature. "The man is deluded. He has no right to anything. My mother was related to this family. What did he say when you told him there was nothing for him?"

Ray met his gaze. "He wasn't happy. He said he'd taken care of your mother and he should share in the inheritance. Then he stormed out muttering something about finding a way to get his fair share."

"No way." Simon got to his feet. He could feel his anger swelling.

"Take it easy. There's no way he can get a penny. Not that there's any pennies to find. The only way he'll get any money is if you give it to him."

Simon rubbed his forehead. "It might be worth it to get him out of my life. Though I'm not sure there's enough money in the world for that."

"Sounds like it hasn't been a very joyful reunion."

Simon filled him in on Buck's treatment of Mikey and Joy. "He can't stay here. I won't subject them to his poison."

"Do you think he'll be back?"

Simon nodded and set his hands on his hips. "You can be sure of it. As long as he thinks there's something to gain. I've got to find a way to make him see he's not welcome here."

Ray stood. "I wish you luck. From what I saw, he's a first-class opportunist."

Simon could add a long list of more unpleasant traits.

By the time Simon turned in for the night, Buck hadn't shown up and Simon began to hope he'd gone on his way since he'd found out there was nothing for him here.

His cell phone jolted him awake. A quick glance at the clock revealed it was two o'clock in the morning.

The name on the screen said Blessing Police Department. A lance of fear brought him fully awake. "Hello."

Simon rolled back onto the bed when the call ended, wishing he'd never answered. Buck had been arrested for drunk and disorderly conduct and he needed bailing out. Simon's first instinct was to let him spend the night in jail. He owed the man nothing. Especially after his treatment of Joy and Mikey.

The bottom line, though, was Buck was his father and deep down Simon knew his mother would want him to do the right thing. Perhaps he could turn this situation to his advantage. He dressed quickly and made a stop at an ATM on his way to the jail. With the right incentive, Buck would be happy to leave Blessing behind forever.

After paying Buck's bail, Simon walked to his truck, his father on his heels. It was all he could do to keep from putting a fist in the man's face.

"Appreciate you coming to my rescue, sonny. That was just a little misunderstanding that got out of hand. You know how those things go."

Simon faced his father. "No. I don't know." He reached into his pocket and pulled out an envelope and handed it to Buck. "Here. Take it and go. I don't want to see you back here again."

Buck flipped through the stack of bills with a smile. "This will hold me for a good while. Think I'll travel on down to the coast and try my luck at those casinos." He saluted and turned to go. "See you in a few weeks, sonny."

Simon started to call out to him but realized it was futile. He'd have to deal with Buck if and when he showed up again. He hoped that wouldn't be until Simon was long gone from Blessing. His surprise visit had cleared up part of his past. It was Buck's selfish pride that had created all the problems, not lack of concern from the townspeople.

He began to wonder what else he'd remembered incorrectly and how it might have contributed to his own perspective on his childhood.

Mikey moaned softly against Joy's side. She held him close, making soothing sounds.

"My hand hurts."

"I know, sweetheart. Let's wait for the medicine to make it feel better." Joy fought off the tidal wave of fear swelling inside her chest. Mikey had awakened around 3:00 a.m. crying. His hand was hurting. It wasn't unusual for the affected hand to ache from time to time. Her son needed physical therapy regularly to keep the hand flexible, and the doctors had told her he would need surgery on it as he grew. He'd already had an operation when he was two. This was the first time he'd been in this much pain and she was getting scared.

A call to his specialist up in Jackson had increased her concern. She was waiting on his return call for new instructions. The phone rang and she answered quickly. The prognosis wasn't good. She paced the room, fighting down the rising panic. She couldn't do this alone. Picking up her phone, she sent a text to Simon, hoping he might be awake. She'd learned to handle many things as a single mom, but this pushed her over the edge.

When Simon didn't respond, she decided to go see him. She didn't want to leave Mikey, but she had to run up to Simon's room and wake him. Mikey had calmed down thanks to the meds. She whispered to him she was going to get Simon then hurried out into the hallway. Simon met her coming from the opposite direction. His worried expression matched her own.

"What's wrong? What's happened?" He took her shoulders in his hands and the warmth and strength collapsed her defenses. She wrapped her arms around him and let the tears fall.

"It's Mikey. His hand is hurting and the doctor says he needs to go to Houston to see the specialist as soon as possible. I need to borrow your truck. My car won't make it that far."

Simon turned her back toward the apartment, keeping his arm across her shoulders. "Where is he?"

Simon went directly to the couch, where the little boy was snuggled under a blanket with Pickles at his feet. "Hey, little buddy. How's it going?"

"I hurt." He held up his left hand and Simon laid his hand on the child's head. "I know, but we're going to get you some help."

Joy stood near them, her heart filled with gratitude for Simon's kindness. She could see that her son felt better just having him here.

Simon moved off a few feet and Joy joined him. "I hate to ask you for your truck, but—"

"No. I'll take you. We'll fly."

Joy shook her head. "I already looked into that and there aren't any flights out of Gulfport until eleven o'clock tomorrow morning."

Simon shook his head and laid his hand on his chest. "No. I'll fly you."

"I don't understand."

"I have my plane at the airport. It's always ready. I can get you to Houston in no time."

It took her a moment to grasp what he'd said. Of course. He was a pilot. What a blessing. She grabbed his hand. "Thank you. Thank you so much."

He smiled and nudged her away. "I'm going to make a few calls and we'll leave as soon as you're ready. I'll be back soon."

By the time Joy had packed a small bag for both of them and made a few calls of her own, she was ready and waiting when Simon returned.

He scooped Mikey into his arms and held him firmly against his chest. "You ready for a trip, buddy?"

"Are we flying in your plane?"

"Yep. Is that okay?"

He nodded with a feeble smile. "Cool."

The ride to the airstrip passed in a blur. Joy sat in the back seat, keeping a hand on Mikey's arm to comfort him. And herself.

The small airplane was sitting lit and running when they pulled up. She had no idea what strings Simon had pulled to make this happen but she would be eternally grateful. He helped her out of the truck and carried Mikey to the plane, then settled him into a cushioned seat behind the cockpit. Joy sat beside him, and even though her thoughts were consumed with Mikey's hand, she was unable to ignore the way Simon commanded the aircraft. For the first time, she understood his desire to start his own business. She'd never witnessed him so comfortable or content as he was flying this plane.

Something about seeing him in his element burrowed deep into her heart. As if she'd been allowed to see a part of his true self he never shared with anyone. It seriously threatened her emotions.

Thankfully, Mikey dozed through most of the flight. Somehow Simon had made arrangements for a vehicle to be waiting for them at the small hangar where they parked to drive them directly to the hospital. It took only minutes for the specialist to meet them and whisk Mikey away for X-rays and tests.

Simon held her hand and she clung to it like a lifeline. "He's so little. He shouldn't have to have surgery at age five."

"Maybe he won't. Let's wait and see."

The next few hours passed in agonizing slowness, thankfully interrupted by brief reassurances from a resident or a nurse. Simon left her side only to get coffee or drinks and she knew he was as anxious about Mikey's prognosis as she was. He truly cared for her son. The thought warmed her heart. This stoic stranger had more love in his heart for her little boy than Mikey's own father had possessed.

It was hard not to love a man who cared like that.

Sitting with him in the waiting room and the hospital chapel, she found a deep sense of connection and security. Having him at her side, comforting her, was something she could happily enjoy for the rest of her life. If it were possible.

She glanced up as an orderly passed by, followed by a police officer who entered one of the rooms. It triggered the memory she'd had before about the officer, only this time it included the man's grim expression and threatening words of some kind before slipping away.

She must have gripped Simon's hand too tightly because he tried to tug his fingers from hers.

"Are you okay?"

She wanted to confide all her fears to him. It was what a woman would do with the man she loved. And she did love him, as pointless as that was. And as dangerous.

"Yes. I'm fine. I just get so scared."

He nodded and slipped his arm around her shoulders. She rested her head against his chest, thankful yet again for his strong presence. Her heart lost another barrier in Simon's arms. It would take only another small step for her to lose it completely.

She closed her eyes against the reality of the situation. How could she even entertain the thought of loving Simon with these memory shards floating around in her head and the niggling impression she knew Simon's name from somewhere? Worse yet, that she might have a deeper connection to his past.

The odd impressions had moved beyond mere frustrating memories. They'd morphed into a ball of perpetual motion, keeping her on edge, her nerves raw, the feelings of fear and dread a constant lump in her throat.

She had to find a way to stop the never-ending cycle.

As soon as Mikey was taken care of, she'd turn all her attention toward uncovering her memories, no matter what that involved. She couldn't continue the way things were.

Simon watched Joy walk Mikey to his bedroom, drawing his first calm breath since Joy's call for help. It had taken all day to run tests on Mikey and determine a diagnosis. Simon couldn't recall the last time he'd prayed so hard or worried so much. He scratched his jaw. No. That wasn't true. He remembered. Once when his mother was dying and again when he'd prayed for Holly and their baby to survive. Only neither prayer had been answered. His mother had died and Holly and the child hadn't survived the accident.

But the Lord had come through for the Duncans and he was deeply grateful. Though he was sure it was the heartfelt pleas of Mikey's mother that the Lord had responded to. He strolled to the window, staring out at the fading light. The doctors had found no reason to keep the boy and determined surgery wasn't necessary at the moment.

Simon didn't understand all the doctors had said, but Joy had appeared relieved and that was enough for him. His chest still felt tight from the tension. The little guy had been almost normal on the flight home, even sitting in the copilot's seat and asking a thousand questions.

Back at the estate, Joy emerged from the bedroom with a look of peace on her pretty face. She met his gaze and his chest tightened another degree with a different kind of tension.

"He wants you to tuck him in."

Simon wasn't sure he'd heard her correctly. "Me?"

She smiled and touched his arm. "He won't sleep until you do."

Mikey was snuggled up with Pickles. He'd had only one request when Joy had announced bedtime—that the dog could sleep with him. Joy had maintained a strict rule about the dog sleeping in his kennel at night, but this time she couldn't say no. He had to admit, the sight of the boy and his dog brought a powerful warmth to his heart.

"Hey, Mr. Simon. Can we fly in your plane again?"

Simon sat on the edge of the bed and scratched behind Pickles's ear. "Of course. Anytime you want."

"I liked being high up. How did you learn to do that?"

"Lots of school. You need to go to sleep, young man. It's been a very long day. How's your hand feeling?"

He held it up. "Good."

The child's resilience never failed to impress him. During his own recuperation from the accident, he'd been less than cooperative. Mikey's bravery shamed him. "Get some sleep, little buddy." He rested his hand on the boy's head then stood.

"Mr. Simon. You'll never go away, will you? You'll stay here forever?"

Simon searched for an answer that would satisfy the child. "I'll be here in the morning."

Mikey smiled and waved. "I love you, Mr. Simon."

Simon's throat clogged with emotion. "Love you, too."

Joy wasn't in the living room when he returned. He found her outside on the porch, her arm wrapped around one of the posts, staring into the fading twilight. She turned when she heard his footsteps on the wooden floor. "I think he'll fall asleep now, as long as he has Pickles with him."

Joy grinned and lowered her chin. "I couldn't say no. He was so brave today. Braver than me."

"Not true. You were amazing."

A sob caught in her throat. "I was a mess. I could

barely think." She caught his gaze. "I can't thank you enough for your help, Simon. I'll never be able to make it up to you. I'll be forever in your debt." She reached up and laid her hand on his scarred cheek. "I've never known anyone with such a big heart and such deep compassion."

Her touch sent a flood of warmth along his nerves. He placed his hand over hers, feeling the fingers flutter beneath his. "I was happy to do it. I'm happy to help you anytime, Joy. I'd do anything for you and Mikey. I care for you both very much."

Joy's eyes glittered with unshed tears. "I couldn't have made it through today without you. I needed your strength and comfort more than you'll know. It's been a long time since I had someone to depend on, someone I could draw courage from. You are such a dear friend to us."

Simon knew in that moment that the last thing he wanted was for Joy to be his friend. She meant far too much to him. He cared too deeply. The affection in her blue eyes shattered his resistance. His gaze focused on her lips. He'd been dreaming about kissing her for a long time. Longer than he'd been willing to admit.

The look in her eyes told him she would welcome him. Her small hand came to rest on his chest over his heart. There was so much he loved about her. He tilted his head then remembered she was his tenant, his employee and a woman he could never have. He placed the kiss on her cheek then stepped back. "You'd better get some sleep. You've had a long day, too. Don't worry about coming to the office tomorrow."

The look of disappointment in her eyes surprised and

buoyed him at the same time. Was she disappointed that he hadn't kissed her the way she wanted?

"I'll be there on time ready to work. Mikey will be back in school, too. I want life to get back to normal for all our sakes."

Normal. Simon wasn't sure he even knew what that was anymore. Nothing had been normal since he'd come to Blessing. And he still wondered if being here was a blessing or a curse.

Joy gently touched her fingertips to his lips then moved past him and went inside the apartment.

His heart beat with a fierce rhythm, propelling the blood through his veins. There was an odd sensation in his chest he couldn't identify. Slowly, he went down the porch steps and walked across the lawn to his own back entrance. He'd always enjoyed being alone in this big old house, but tonight he was struck by the size and the emptiness of it. He realized that his life had been empty for a long time and he didn't want to feel that way anymore. He didn't want to be alone.

In his office, his gaze went immediately to Joy's alcove. He didn't feel alone when he was with her. Moving forward, however, meant leaving behind the things he'd loved and cherished, and closing the door on those memories would be cruel and callous.

His cell phone vibrated in his pocket, reminding him that he'd had it on silent since they'd arrived at the hospital. He frowned when he saw Ray's name appear.

"What's up?"

"I just got a call from Millie Gayton. Your little pal Arlo is in jail. Seems he got himself caught up in a mess with some other boys."

So much for keeping the kid out of trouble. "And she called you?"

"I'm the only lawyer she knows. You want me to handle this or do you want to get involved?"

Simon exhaled a tired breath. First his dad, now Arlo. "I'll meet you at the jail."

By the time he and Ray had arranged for Arlo's bail and taken him home, it was nearing ten o'clock. He'd promised Arlo's grandmother that he would have a talk with the boy and try to set him straight.

He doubted he could make a difference in the young man's attitude. He remembered being sixteen and unwilling to listen to anyone. He needed someone with more wisdom and understanding than he possessed. Someone like Joy.

She'd been a blessing to him—perhaps she could be one to Arlo, as well.

Simon walked into his office the next morning shocked to find Joy behind his desk. "I know you said you wanted to come back to work today, but isn't this a little early even for you? Did something happen? Is Mikey all right?"

"He's fine. He's sound asleep. I came to check on you. I saw you leave late last night and I was worried."

Simon lowered himself into a chair. He wasn't looking forward to telling Joy about the boy's situation. "I had to bail Arlo out of jail. He got caught up in some mischief with that group of boys he hangs with."

"Oh no. I thought he was keeping busy helping at the theater and making new friends."

"Me, too. But apparently, the call of the old crew

was too strong. They decided to deface the statue of Sergeant Croft in the square. I have no idea why they would target the monument but they did."

"I can't believe this. What will happen to him?"

Simon shrugged. "That's up to the judge. He has to appear in court in a few days. I'm responsible for him until then. Ray will do his best to get the charges dropped but he's doubtful. The best he thinks he can do is get community service."

"Why would Arlo do such a thing? It seems so out of character."

Simon met her gaze. "Because belonging to the group is the most important thing in your life at that age. Thumbing your nose at authority makes you feel grown up, like you have some control over your life."

"You're speaking from experience."

He nodded. "It's a powerful need, belonging and feeling you matter." Joy stood and came to his side, resting her hand on his shoulder.

"If anyone can get through to him, it's you. He respects you, Simon. He'll listen."

He looked up into her eyes and saw trust and belief. It humbled him. "Would you be there when I talk to him tomorrow afternoon? He's supposed to be here after school."

"Of course. What are you going to say to him?"

Simon shook his head. "I have no idea. I'm just going to wing it, I guess. I'm hoping you'll have some words of wisdom to add. He likes you."

Joy blew out a doubtful breath. "Getting through to teenage boys isn't easy."

He raised his brows. "You're talking to an expert."

She gave him an encouraging smile. "I'll be here. Maybe between us we can set him straight."

Simon reached for her hand searching for courage to express what he was feeling.

"Hey, sonny, I'm back. Did you miss me? Oh, I didn't know you and the missus were busy."

Joy gripped his shoulder. He stood and faced his father. "You're not welcome here. I told you to go."

Buck held up his hands in a gesture of submission. "I'm going. I'm going. First thing in the morning. Got me a ride to Mobile with a friend." He scratched his chin. "But I need a place to crash tonight, so I figured we'd spend one more night together for old times' sake."

A swell of anger rushed through his system. "There's a motel out by the interstate. I'm sure they have room."

"That costs money. Besides, I like that nice soft bed in that room of yours. I thought we could have breakfast together the three of us. I'd like to get to know your wife."

Joy spoke up. "I'm not his wife."

Buck chuckled. "That's what you keep saying but from my viewpoint, I see there's something going on between you two."

Simon took a threatening step toward his father but Joy held him back. "I need to get back to Mikey. We'll talk about things in the morning." She gave him an encouraging smile. "Everything will be back to normal after tomorrow."

He leaned close and whispered in her ear, "Thank you. I'll fix this and make sure my dad goes for good."

He watched her go, her words of tender understanding covering his rising anger like a soothing balm. She had a knack for keeping him on an even keel, even in the worst situations. They were a good complement to one another. Too bad there was no real future for them.

Chapter Eleven

Joy took one last sip of her morning coffee, lingering in the coolness of the breeze on her porch and the blissful quiet. She'd dropped off Mikey at school early and returned home for one more cup before going to work. Truth was, she was putting off going to the office as long as possible. She didn't want to encounter Buck Baker again. He was a thoroughly unpleasant man. The obvious animosity between him and Simon was hard to watch. Buck had said he'd be leaving this morning and she prayed he would be for Simon's sake.

She had a better understanding why Simon hated being in Blessing. In the short time they'd worked together, he'd had to face multiple emotional reunions. None of which she'd been able to help him with. She wished there was something she could do to give him a break from the constant obstacles that kept plaguing him. The failed sales, the appearance of his father, Arlo's trouble and Mikey's emergency were all taking a toll. Not to mention the loss of his investor.

Carrying her mug to the sink, she then rinsed it and

set it on the counter, her gaze falling on the flyer for the Blessing Bicentennial Hot Air Balloon Fest. Perfect. What could be more calming than the breathtaking sight of colorful balloons floating in the air by day and the beauty of them glowing softly in the night? Mikey would love it and she felt sure as a pilot Simon would, too.

Besides, after their meeting with Arlo this afternoon, they'd both need some way to relax. She wasn't looking forward to talking to her young friend. She'd prayed about it all night and prayed for Miss Millie. The last thing she needed was to have Arlo mixed up with the law.

Walking briskly toward the office, Joy slowed when she heard angry voices. Buck and Simon.

"This ends now. Don't bother coming back because this place will be sold and boarded up. No more hospitality. I'll be gone and I don't want to see you ever again. Is that clear?"

"Now, sonny, don't get yourself all fired up. We'll always be related and there's not a thing you can do to change that."

Joy held her breath as Buck strolled out of the office and gave her a wink before walking out the front door. Slowly she entered the office. Simon was sitting at his desk, head cradled in his hands.

"Are you all right?" He raised his head and she saw the torment in his dark eyes. "I heard the, um…" She waved her hand.

He intertwined his fingers in front of his chin. "I don't see the man for years and now I can't get rid of him."

"Do you think he's gone for good now?" She hoped

so. Simon had enough on his plate without having to deal with his belligerent parent.

"At least until the money runs out."

"Did you mean what you said, about boarding up the house? I mean, have you received an offer?"

A small smile moved Simon's lips. "No. That was for my father's benefit. If he thinks I'll be here, then he'll keep coming back for more."

The sense of relief that rushed through her was surprising. She set it aside and went forward with her plan. "I have an invitation for you."

Simon's eyes lit up. "Whatever it is, I'm in."

She moved around the desk and handed him the colorful flyer. "It starts tonight with the balloon glow at the high school. I think Mikey would love to see them all lit up. So would I."

He smiled up at her. "That makes three of us. It's a date. I'll drive. Do you want to eat there? I haven't had a good funnel cake in a long time. Or a carnival hot dog." He gently touched her hand. "Mostly I like spending time with my two favorite people."

Joy's heart swelled with happiness. She felt the same way. However, before they could enjoy the evening, they had a bigger issue to deal with. "What time is Arlo due?"

"Around three."

"I'll make arrangements for Mikey to stay at day care a little longer. I wish we didn't have to do this. I've known Arlo a long time. He's a good kid. I don't understand how he got into this mess. Millie is so upset."

Simon nodded. "That's one reason I want to talk to the boy. I'm hoping we can stop this behavior from escalating. I'm picking him up from school. I don't want to leave any room for him to change his mind and find something more exciting to do."

"Wise move. Facing the music is never easy when you're a teenager."

Simon grinned knowingly. "Exactly. I would gladly have rather joined the foreign legion than face my mom and one of her talks."

A short while later, Simon knocked on her door. She'd come to the apartment to let Pickles outside. By the look on his face, he was dreading this confrontation as much as she was. "Is he here?"

"He's waiting in my office. I thought we should go together."

Joy didn't challenge his statement. She knew he was wanting moral support. So was she. The knot of anxiety in her chest was pressing against her lungs, impeding her breathing.

They stepped into the office to find Arlo seated at Simon's desk, looking at his computer. Joy swallowed her surprise and glanced at her boss. He was obviously irritated.

"Arlo."

The hard tone in Simon's voice brought the teen to his feet, bumping his knees and scurrying from behind the large desk. "I'm sorry. I wasn't snooping, honest. I saw the pictures of planes and I wanted a closer look, so I just…"

Simon moved forward and pointed to the sofa and chairs at the end of the room. Joy suspected Simon didn't want this talk to take place with a formal desk between them. Better to approach it like a simple discussion between friends.

Arlo's cheeks were still flushed from embarrassment as he took a seat on the sofa. Joy's heart ached for him. Simon leaned forward in his chair, resting his arms on his knees in a relaxed pose. "I thought we should talk about your situation."

Arlo swallowed and nodded, his dark eyes wary. "Yes, sir."

Joy wished she could give him a hug. He looked miserable. However, he'd brought this on himself.

Simon waited patiently. "Start from the beginning."

Arlo glanced between them. "I, uh, the guys wanted to hang out, so they picked me up and we went downtown."

"What did you do?"

He squirmed, rubbing the back of his hand. "Nothing, just walked around. You know, stuff like that."

"How did the vandalism start?"

Arlo looked confused. Joy explained softly, "Why did you decide to spray paint the statue?"

He glanced at Simon then lowered his head. "It wasn't my idea. Troy had some spray cans and he said it would be fun."

"And you thought so, too?" Simon asked.

"No. I mean…" Arlo shrugged. "They were all fired up and I couldn't tell them to stop."

Simon leaned back and crossed his legs. "Arlo, were these boys taunting you? Were they pushing you to go along for some reason?"

"Well, uh, I guess so. Maybe."

Joy bit her lip. From the shocked expression on the boy's face, Simon must have hit on the truth.

"How long have you been friends with these boys, son?"

Arlo rubbed his palms along his thighs. "Since the diner burned."

Joy couldn't stand it another moment. She moved beside Arlo on the sofa and slipped her arm across his shoulders. "What's really going on? I know this isn't who you are. What aren't you telling us? It's okay. We're here to help, not get you in more trouble. But you have to realize you've disappointed a lot of people, especially your grandmother. She needs your help now, not more trouble."

Tears filled the teen's eyes as he started to explain. He told them how he'd met the three boys at school and how they'd started saying he was working for Simon, so he could steal things from the house. When they learned of his involvement in the theater, they started to tease him and threaten to tell everyone he liked to dress up and wear makeup. Arlo wiped his eyes. "I tried to tell them I was building things and using cool tools, but they didn't believe me."

Simon nodded, rubbing his chin. "I spoke with your gram and she said your grades are starting to fall. Is that because of your association with these boys?" Arlo nodded and Simon exhaled a deep sigh. "So they mean more to you than your grandmother does?"

Joy squeezed the boy's arm, her heart stinging. She knew Simon wasn't being deliberately harsh. Arlo needed to have his eyes opened to what he was doing, but she hated that he had to endure this.

"No, but they're my friends. They said I could be one of them if I proved myself."

"And to do that you had to deface a cherished symbol of the town? Let me ask you this. When the police showed up, what did they do?"

Arlo swallowed. "They, uh, ran off. Except Judd. He got caught, too."

Simon leaned forward again, capturing Arlo's attention. "So they left you to take the blame. Does that sound like something friends would do? Believe me, they aren't your friends. Real friends don't encourage their pals to commit crimes. You're their pet target. They've chosen you to degrade and humiliate for their own amusement, and they'll keep doing this until you stand up to them or walk away. They're bullies and their only goal is to be as mean and spiteful to others as they can."

Arlo frowned and gave Simon a sour look. "How do you know? You're rich. You never had people messing with you."

Joy braced for Simon's response, uncertain how he would address the accusation. She'd forgotten how much he and Arlo had in common.

"I was a poor kid whose dad was the town drunk. I had plenty of bullies pushing me around. Ask your grandmother. She knew my mom and she'll know all about my bad behavior growing up."

"What did you do about the bullies? How did you stop them?"

Simon rubbed his jaw. "I went to live with my sister and I had a chance to start over. I made new friends and learned carpentry and everything started to change."

Arlo's tone was confrontational. "Great for you but I can't move away."

"No, but you can learn something new."

"Huh?"

Joy searched Simon's expression for some clue to his idea. She suspected he had a plan to steer the boy back to the straight and narrow but he hadn't confided in her.

"How would you like to learn to fly a plane?"

Arlo glanced at her then at Simon. "Yeah, cool, but I can't afford it."

"I'll teach you. But you have to agree on a few conditions. You keep your grades up, you cut yourself loose from those so-called friends, and you stay involved in the theater group. Think you can do that?"

Arlo nodded, a small grin on his face. "Are you for real? You'll teach me to fly?"

"I will. But you need to know there's book work involved. There are principles of flight to learn and a lot of other things. It's not like a car. You don't just crank the engine and steer."

"That's okay, I can learn stuff pretty fast." He looked between them. "So, you're not firing me from the grass-cutting job?"

"No."

He sighed loudly. "Good. Gram would kill me for sure."

Joy grinned. "I wouldn't blame her. She's out of work and struggling with only one hand. She needs you to be there for her. It might take a while to regain her trust, however."

Arlo hung his head. "Yeah. I just wanted to be one of the guys, you know."

Simon stood. "Believe me. I know exactly how you feel."

Arlo came to his feet. "What about all the legal stuff? Am I going to jail? Who'll take care of Gram?"

Simon rested a hand on the teen's shoulder. "Mr. Ray doesn't think it'll come to that, but you'll probably get some community service to complete."

Arlo faced Simon, his shoulders squared, his chin level. "Why are you doing this for me? I'm just some kid who mows your lawn."

Simon caught her gaze briefly. "Someone helped me once. I'm just paying it forward."

"Thanks, Mr. Simon. Miss Joy. I'll work hard to make this right. Honest."

Joy gave him a little hug. "I know you will. Why don't you go and wait for me in my car and I'll drive you home. We'll explain all this to your gram."

Joy watched the boy leave then slipped her hand in Simon's. "Do you think we got through to him?"

"I do. He's a good kid. It's just too easy to fall in with the wrong crowd."

"Are you really going to teach him to fly?"

"Of course." He grinned, his eyes twinkling. "You want to learn, too? I'd love to teach you."

She shook her head, her heart melting at the compassionate nature of this man she admired. Resting her hand on his shoulder, she stood on tiptoe and kissed his cheek, intending it to be a friendly gesture, but her aim was off and her lips landed at the edge of his mouth. The resulting effect was something else entirely. She looked into Simon's dark eyes and saw affection, attraction. Her heart raced. He slipped his arm around her waist and pulled her close, his free hand tilting her chin upward. She should stop this from happening but she didn't want to. She'd wondered about his kiss for too long.

He whispered her name and her bones melted. His kiss was light, gentle and full of warmth. She allowed herself to let go and embrace the closeness and sense of belonging.

Too quickly the kiss ended, the cool air a rude intruder between them. She stepped back, her heart pinching at the look on Simon's face. He looked stunned and confused. He obviously thought the kiss was a mistake. She stepped away, brushing her hair from her cheek. "I'd better go, uh… Arlo is, uh, waiting for me."

"Joy."

She ignored the way the sound of her name on his lips softened her heart and quickened her steps. She should have been stronger, she should have resisted temptation. Now things would be awkward between them again. That seemed to be the nature of their relationship.

She wondered if their plans for the balloon glow would go forward or would he make an excuse to stay home?

Would there ever be a time when they were on the same page?

Simon let his gaze travel over the colorful sights spread out before him at the high school. The parking lot had been turned into a small carnival with food stalls, rides and games. Mikey was captivated by all of it. He'd already ridden with Simon on the merry-go-round and the three of them had been scrunched together in the Scrambler.

He couldn't remember the last time he'd had so much fun, despite the complaining of his stomach over the heavy food he'd consumed. It was a small price to pay for spending this time with Joy and Mikey. Watching the happiness on Joy's face and the excitement on Mikey's allowed him to pretend he was part of a family. He just had to remember he wasn't. His family was gone.

He'd almost begged off from coming to the event. The kiss he'd shared with Joy had unsettled him profoundly. He'd been unprepared for the way the kiss had drawn her deeper into his emotions. She'd pulled away, and the look of surprise on her face had forced him to realize that he'd overstepped his boundaries. She was obviously unhappy that he'd been so forward.

He'd decided to follow through with their date and he'd been very relieved when she greeted him at the door as if nothing had happened. He'd been looking forward to the balloon glow more than he'd realized. And so far, he hadn't been disappointed.

Willa came toward them carrying a large bag over her shoulder. "Isn't this wonderful?"

Joy smiled. "What have you got there?"

"Goodies. I've spent a fortune on 200th birthday souvenirs. T-shirts, mugs, plastic cups and jewelry. Look." She held up a necklace with the image of the Blessing Bridge. "I got you one, too."

"Did you get me something?" Mikey looked up with a smile.

"Not yet. I thought you might like to come with me to pick out a shirt or a toy."

"Can we get something for Pickles, too?"

"Absolutely." Mikey took Willa's hand.

Joy chuckled. "The balloon glow is starting in a few minutes."

"I'll bring him over when we're done."

They agreed on a meeting place then Willa and Mikey walked off.

Simon took Joy's hand in his, marveling at how right it felt. "You're very blessed, Joy. You have so many people who love you and care for you. I envy that."

She squeezed his hand. "So do you, Simon. You have me and Mikey, and Willa and Ray, and a lot of other people if you'd let them in."

"Why are you so optimistic?"

"Why are you so pessimistic?"

He chuckled and squeezed her hand. "Let's go claim our spot for the glow. I know you're looking forward to seeing all the balloons lighting up the night."

Joy exhaled a soft sigh as they watched the colorful balloon envelopes being inflated, the propane tanks hissing as they released the gas into the balloons. "Aren't they beautiful? So many styles, colors and shapes. It must be wonderful riding in one of them. Oh, look, there's a Mississippi balloon shaped like an alligator."

"Would you like to go up?"

Joy's eyes lit up. "Oh, yes. But I'd be too scared. There's no steering, no controls. You're at the mercy of the wind. Anything could happen."

"True, but in the hands of an experienced pilot you'd

be perfectly safe. Would you go up in a basket with someone you trusted? Say, like me?"

Her eyes widened. "You can fly a hot-air balloon?"

"I can. I have a license and everything. I can arrange a flight tomorrow if you'd like." The smile she gave him confirmed his suspicions. He'd lost his heart to this woman and he doubted if he'd get it back. Joy turned and faced the field of balloons, her back only inches from his chest. He rested his hands on her shoulders, enjoying her nearness. He never appreciated the beauty of the glowing envelopes as much as he did now. Having someone to share the experience with made everything more special.

"I hope Mikey is seeing this." Joy smiled up at him.

"Willa won't let him miss it."

They strolled along the perimeter of the ball field, stopping by the Mississippi balloon to take a selfie. When they continued on, Simon took her hand again. She smiled up at him and he smiled back. She'd made it easy to smile, to appreciate all the things around him that he'd been blind to before. "Thank you for inviting me tonight. I haven't had this much fun in a long time."

"I'm glad. It's nice to see you relaxed and happy. For a long time I didn't think you knew how."

He nodded. "I had no reason to enjoy life." He caught her gaze. "I do now."

"Hey, Miss Joy. Mr. Simon." Arlo walked up with an attractive girl at his side. He introduced her as Brianna.

"Will we see you at the theater tomorrow night? We need to finish up those benches for the third act."

"Yes, sir. Brianna is coming, too."

"Good. We need all the help we can get." Simon

watched the pair walk away. Joy squeezed his hand. "Something wrong? Why the frown?"

"Not sure. I was so concerned about him staying clear of that gang, maybe I should have steered him clear of girls, too."

Joy laughed. "Good luck with that. I hope Arlo sticks to your plan. I want him to succeed."

"Me, too. I've already ordered his flight instruction books. I'm looking forward to teaching him. I'm surprised to see him here, though. I expected Miss Millie to ground him for life."

"She said this was his last big outing. Starting tomorrow he'll be too busy to go gallivanting."

"Mommy."

Simon released Joy's hand as Mikey and Willa came toward them. His hand felt strangely cold and empty. He watched as Joy and Willa chatted and Mikey showed off his new treasures. Something about Joy made him feel lighter, stronger, as if he drew strength from her inherent joy. She truly embodied her name.

A couple strolled past them hand in hand. The woman was obviously pregnant. A quick shaft of pain pierced Simon's heart, reminding him of what he'd lost. He glanced at the field now filled with glowing hot-air balloons. What was he doing? He swallowed the lump in his throat. He was pretending to be a family, allowing himself to care for two people who could never replace what he'd lost. And he couldn't risk losing again. He would never survive another loss like that.

It was time to back off and regain control of his emotions before he made a very big mistake for everyone involved.

Chapter Twelve

Joy watched Simon carry a sleeping Mikey to his room and laid him down. She quickly removed his clothes and covered him up, then joined Simon in the living room. "He is completely worn-out, but he had so much fun."

"He's not alone. I'm ready to turn in myself."

Joy studied him as she drew near. Something had changed. She wasn't sure what. Through the whole evening, he'd been relaxed and amiable. Then for no reason she could find, he'd withdrawn and grown somber. She wanted to ask him about it but now was not the time. They were both tired. She'd wait until the morning and gauge his mood after his coffee.

"Good night, Simon." She smiled, resisting the urge to touch his arm.

He barely glanced at her. "Night. See you Monday."

He walked out and Joy's concern grew. Monday? Was he going out of town or simply planning on avoiding her for the rest of the weekend? What had happened? He'd reacted like a hermit crab, pulling back into his shell and refusing to come out.

After pouring a glass of tea, she stepped out onto the porch and sat in the rocker. She was exhausted, but it was too early to turn in and her mind was puzzling over Simon's mood swing. She was afraid it was because of the kiss they'd shared.

He'd been opening up to her more and more about his past and his feelings, but now he'd fallen back into his reclusive mode. More than anything she wished she could take away his hurt and his anger. He was stuck in the grieving process and unable, or unwilling, to move on. There was so much good in him, so much kindness and love. He was afraid to risk his heart again and she understood that fear.

Fatigue was taking over and she allowed her mind to drift. A flash of memory flared with stunning clarity. Snow thick as a curtain, falling sideways. A sense of being propelled forward. Spinning and sliding then nothing.

Sweat popped out on her skin. Her heart raced. She rubbed her temple. Why did she only get bits and pieces of the accident? Why couldn't she open that locked box and see the whole event?

Maybe she wasn't taking the right approach. Maybe she needed to do the thing she'd been denying all these years. Asking God to reveal her past, to restore her memory, so she could understand what had happened. Mainly she needed to understand the fear whenever she tried to remember and why Simon seemed to be part of it.

The weather was turning cloudy and the wind was picking up the Monday morning when she made her way down the path to the bridge after dropping Mikey off at school. Her nerves were jumping as she stood in the middle of the bridge. This was a prayer she'd been avoiding for years. Her spotty recollection of the accident had been a concern, but there'd been no reason to worry about it. It hadn't affected her life in any way.

It was different now. The memories were emerging like seeds pushing through the soil, determined to find the sunlight. Each one sprouted with a new fear that she didn't understand. But she knew she had to find the answers, no matter what she discovered.

The autumn wind blew leaves from the trees and sent them spiraling down into the pond, reminding her that time was passing, not only for her but for the bridge land. Closing her eyes, she opened her heart and prayed for direction, for the bridge, for her tangled thoughts and emotions, and clarity for her spotty memory. She'd reached a breaking point. She couldn't continue with all these doubts and fears. The constant anxiety and stress were making her ill. *Please, Lord, show me the truth. Restore my memory.*

Strengthened by her time in prayer, Joy entered the office prepared to have a conversation with Simon only to find he wasn't there. Her disappointment lingered through lunch with Willa. They'd met at the Waterway Restaurant on the Riverbank Walk.

"I have to know, Willa. I can't keep living with this irrational fear every time I try to remember. Why do I have this sense of dread?"

"Because you are afraid to remember the accident. I'm sure it was a terrifying thing to go through. It's only natural you wouldn't want to relive something like that."

Joy nodded. Willa made a good point, but Joy couldn't shake the feeling that there was more to it all.

"Think about it. These things you learned about Simon are connected to the accident, right? But all that means is that they trigger your memories of that night. That doesn't mean Simon has any part in the event." Willa reached across the table and patted her hand. "I think you need to do some digging and find out what really happened that night and stop imagining the worst. I found this for you. You can request your accident report online."

Joy took the note. She'd asked the Lord for answers. This might be the first step to finding them. "I know. I nearly applied a while back but I chickened out."

"Then I'm glad I made the move for you." Willa sat down beside her. "I know this is scary, kiddo, but you can't keep avoiding the truth. You know that."

Joy nodded. Hadn't she told Simon the same thing about hiding from his pain? She stared at the note. Her pulse began to race. But was she ready to learn the truth? What if the truth was worse than she'd feared?

Willa patted her hand. "Will you do it?"

Joy nodded. She had to face this sooner or later. Now was as good a time as any.

Ray looked up as Simon entered his office. "Did we have an appointment?"

"No. I just thought I'd stop by and check on things." He knew his friend could see right through him. Simon was at loose ends and trying to kill time.

Ray frowned. "Things? Like what?"

Simon shrugged. "The inheritance, the properties. You know."

Ray grinned. "Sorry. Nothing to report. Sheila would have been in touch if there were." He leaned his arms on the desk. "Did you have a nice time at the balloon glow last night?"

"How did you know I was there?"

"There were a lot of people there. Like me and Virginia."

"Oh. Right."

"You and Joy looked very happy together."

"We weren't together. We were just…"

"In the same place at the same time. Right. How's Mikey? I heard about your midnight flight to Texas."

Simon shook his head. "Do you know everything that goes on around here?"

"It's a small town. Hard to keep secrets."

One of the many reasons he'd kept a low profile when he came here. "He's fine. No surgery needed at the moment. He was a brave little kid. Joy's an amazing mother."

"Sounds like you're in love with her."

"What? Of course not. I couldn't be. I mean, we're friends and coworkers, but that's all." Even after the kiss they'd shared, his mind and heart denied that statement. He was in love with her but he could never act upon it. He'd gotten entangled with Joy and Mikey without realizing it. He'd had to be strong for Joy's sake at the hospital, but his insides felt as if he'd swallowed shards of glass. Thinking of little Mikey undergoing surgery and the pain he would have to endure had been torturous. How did Joy cope day after day? He looked at Ray, who was staring with a curious expression. "No. That's not going to happen. She's just a good friend."

"Hmm. Really? What about Mikey? Is he just a friend, too?"

Simon couldn't help but smile. "He's my little buddy. A great kid. He was so brave at the hospital. The doctors said he never cried once during all the tests."

"So what happens when you leave here?"

"They stay."

"And the friendship ends. Just like that? You ride off into the sunset like a lone cowboy on your beloved horse? And what about Arlo? You were going to give him flying lessons. What happens to him?"

Simon dragged his hand over his cheek. He'd forgotten about that. "I'll hire someone to teach him."

Ray snickered. "It won't be the same. He looks up to you. He wants to learn from you, not some stranger."

"I'll work it out. I'm not leaving yet."

"Good. Then there's plenty of time for you to come to your senses."

Simon mulled over Ray's observations on the drive back home. His friend had a valid point. One Simon didn't want to examine too closely. He would leave Blessing at some point. Technically he could leave now, except he wasn't ready to say goodbye to Joy and Mikey. The trip to the hospital had drawn them deeper into his affections, and his life. Sitting in the waiting room with Joy and holding her hand had shattered the barrier around his heart completely. He realized he loved little Mikey as if he were his own son. But he'd had a child. And a family. Loving someone else would be a betrayal. But how would he say goodbye to them? He just needed a little time to let his emotions settle down.

His cell phone rang as he walked into his office. Sheila. She was excited to tell him that she'd had interest in the hotel. Just a nibble but she believed they were very serious. He sat down at his desk. He should feel elated. Finally, his plan was coming together. First the McCray building, then the theater and now the hotel. He could leave Blessing today and start organizing his business.

Of course, now he needed to wait to see what developed with the hotel offer. That should give him time to disengage from things here in Blessing and prepare to go home. The thought didn't fill him with the satisfaction it had in the past. Arlo added a new wrinkle to the picture. He didn't like breaking promises but he had no choice.

Somehow, he had to cut himself loose from the roots he'd started to grow here and move on before they shackled him in Blessing forever.

Joy opened the email from Sheila Monday morning, her heart sinking as she read the supposedly good news. Someone had made an official offer on the hotel. A local, but Joy didn't recognize the name. This was the final piece that Simon had been waiting for. He would be free and probably very eager to hop in his plane and fly away home.

She brushed her hair back from her face. She should be happy for him. It was what he wanted. He'd made no bones about it. Closing her eyes, she fought the sting of tears forming. She didn't want him to go.

Something had happened to her during their adventure to Houston and back. There'd been a seismic shift in their relationship. At least for her. Having Simon to lean on through the night had been a godsend. Getting them to Houston quickly had saved her sanity. It had also uncovered her true feelings.

She loved Simon Baker.

She knew he cared for her and for Mikey, but he was still trapped in grief and resentment. If she could only show him he had to let go of his anger and forgive the person driving the car that night. She wanted to free him to move on and be happy again.

After tucking Mikey into bed that evening, Joy curled up on the sofa with a pad and pencil and began to write down the pieces of memory she could recall and put them in order. The resulting random picture made no sense. She stood and went to the kitchen and stared out at the yard. It had been over a week since she'd requested the accident report. Until it arrived, she was left to sort through her patchy memory as best she could.

Her thoughts turned to the other situation she could do little about. The Blessing Bridge.

Time was nearly up and Simon had still not made a decision. Mayor Russell had contacted him personally with an appeal. For reasons Joy couldn't understand, her boss was refusing to listen to any plea or argument.

She arrived at work the next day tired from wrestling with her past and worrying over the future. Thankfully, Simon was in and out all day, which gave her plenty of time to catch up on her work.

It was nearly quitting time when she checked her email and found the accident report waiting to be opened. She stared at the screen, heart in her throat and her palms suddenly clammy, terrified of what she might find. She'd wondered about the accident for the last three years but had never bothered to read it, too afraid of what it might reveal. Her life had been filled with healing and surviving and providing for her son. Now she might have the answers her brain had blocked out.

What should she do? If she deleted the report, she'd never have to know what really happened. But living with the doubts wasn't an option any longer. Not with Simon in her life now.

Her courage rose and fell for ten minutes before she finally opened the file. Slowly she scanned the document. Date. Name. Location. Make and model of car. The next section concerned the vehicle she'd struck. Her gaze froze on the name of the owner. Simon J. Baker. She gasped. The image she'd seen of his name printed in a box was right in front of her. This was where she'd seen it. His name on the narrow lines of the accident report.

She was the driver. She'd hit his car and killed his family.

Her throat seized up and her stomach heaved, sending acid bile into her mouth. How could this be? She covered her mouth to stop the scream from escaping. Her head throbbed in pain, blurring her vision. No. It couldn't be true. Her mind cried out in horror. A sob escaped her throat. Tears filled her eyes. She couldn't be responsible for the loss of Simon's family. She buried her face in her hands. This had to be a mistake. How could she live with this guilt? She glanced toward the office, thankful he wasn't there. She couldn't face him, knowing what she'd done.

Simon would hate her if he found out. Pain like a sharp knife plunged into her mind. Her stomach churned and her face grew warm. She hurried to the bathroom and put cold water on her forehead. If only she could remember. She had the facts in front of her but she still couldn't remember that night.

Back at her computer, she willed herself to recall that night. It was February. The storm had descended on the city suddenly, creating chaos everywhere. She'd worked late. The storm was raging as she'd driven home. Forecasters had warned of black ice and a whiteout. She remembered a flash of light then waking up in the hospital. Most of her time in the hospital was a blur, too.

Joy scraped her fingertips across her scalp, tears threatening behind her eyes. Why couldn't she remember? She'd learned to live with the gaps because they didn't seem important. But now, knowing Simon and the things he'd said, she had to know. Now it was vital that she remember everything.

For Simon's sake.

Simon entered his office and went directly to his desk. He'd met with Sheila to go over the hotel offer. The buyer had some concerns Simon might have to deal with before they could agree on a price but was very interested. Simon inhaled a deep breath, taking in the faint whiff of Joy's perfume. He always knew when Joy was in her alcove. The office had an energy and a warmth that was missing when she wasn't here.

He stood and walked around his desk to share the

news about the hotel. Joy suddenly appeared in front of him and his smile quickly turned to alarm. She had a look of horror on her face and she was as pale as a ghost. "What's wrong? What's happened?"

She gasped, her eyes widening in fear. Her hand clutched her shirt at her stomach. Her other hand was fisted tight at her side and she was shaking. He took a step toward her and she yelped and backed away. "I've got to go. I've got to…" She looked around like a trapped animal. "Mikey is…alone." She spun and hurried away.

Simon went after her but she'd already disappeared around the corner. "Joy!" He debated whether to go after her then decided it might be better to give her some space. He'd check on her later, after she'd had time to calm down.

Back at his desk, he tried to figure out what had upset her. She would have told him if it was Mikey. She knew how much he cared for the boy. Was she ill? Could it have been another one of her headaches like before? It was the look of fear and horror he'd seen in her eyes that he couldn't shake. It tore at his heart. He couldn't stand seeing her so upset. But he had no idea what had caused it.

He managed to stay busy for an hour before worry took over. Joy's behavior couldn't be set aside any longer. He'd hoped she would return after she calmed down and explain, but she hadn't. Time to go to the apartment and see for himself. As he walked past her alcove, the thought occurred to him that maybe she'd received some news that had upset her. Perhaps something had happened to her parents. He knew they were retired and living in Arizona.

Her computer screen was still dark, so he tapped the space bar. A document appeared. He scanned the page. An accident report from the Charlotte Police Department. Joy's auto wreck, which had caused her concussion and resulting headaches. He sat down, his gaze locked on a printed copy of the report on the screen. Slowly, he read through the page.

Pain and anger sliced through his entire being. The other car was his. Joy was the driver that night. She was the one who'd crashed through the intersection and killed his family.

Darkness descended on his mind. His heart refused to beat and his lungs froze. It couldn't be Joy. Impossible. He sorted through the things she'd told him. Joy had lived in Charlotte. He shook his head. No. It was too far-fetched, too impossible to accept. There had to be another explanation.

His shock gave way to anger then rage. Did she know? Had she always known and never said anything? He didn't want to believe she was capable of such duplicity, but he the proof was in front of his eyes. The report didn't lie. He scanned it again. His name, his address.

He set his jaw, struggling to control his rising fury. How could she do this to him? How could she keep silent? How could she be the one he'd hated all this time?

Shoving back from the desk, Simon stood and stormed out of the office and marched to the apartment and banged on the door. "Joy? I found the report. Joy. How could you?" He pounded harder. "It was you!

You drove your car into that intersection. You took everything from me. Joy!"

His fist caused the door to rattle. "Open up. You owe me an explanation." Out of patience, he grabbed the doorknob and entered the apartment. He sensed something wrong immediately. It was silent. Too silent. "Joy!"

A different kind of alarm started to seep into his being. He looked into the bedrooms. Clothes and a few toys were scattered on Mikey's bed. Joy's room looked much the same. As if they'd left in a hurry. In the kitchen he noticed that Pickles's crate was missing. A quick look outside confirmed his suspicions. Her car was gone. Joy and Mikey had left.

An admission of guilt? Was she running from him, afraid of what he might do?

Realization sent him onto a kitchen chair. Was she really afraid of him? Was that why she'd run away? Had he scared her that much? He needed an explanation, but he would never harm her. He loved her. He leaned back and stared at the ceiling. He loved her, but how could he when she was the reason he'd lost Holly and the baby?

His mind refused to accept that Joy was the driver of the car. Bowing his head, he tried to pray but his mind refused to form words. Slowly, he became aware of the silence in the apartment. The lack of life. The people who had given it energy were gone. That realization hurt as much as the accident report.

Joy and Mikey were gone. The hole in his heart turned as cold as a glacier. He didn't want to go on without them. But he couldn't go on knowing what Joy had done. He had to see her and get some answers. Pulling out his phone, he called Willa. It was the first place Joy would go. The call went to voice mail. He tried twice more with the same result.

The small kitchen closed in around him. What did he do now? Did he find Joy or cut her out of his life? Did he demand an explanation or walk away? None of the options seemed satisfying.

He had nowhere to turn.

He'd never felt so lost and abandoned in his life.

Chapter Thirteen

Joy pulled another tissue from the nearly empty box and wiped her eyes, then took the two pain pills Willa handed her knowing they wouldn't do any good. The pain she was feeling couldn't be eased with medication. She swallowed them to satisfy her cousin. "Thank you."

Willa joined her on the sofa. "I don't know what to say. I should have paid more attention to your suspicions about some connection to Simon. It all seemed so fantastic. Too big a coincidence to have actually happened."

"I don't know what to do. I can't face him. He hates me and I can't blame him. I'm responsible for him losing…" Sobs erupted again. Her heart tried to beat in spite of the giant clamp that bound it.

"Hush. Remember it was an accident. The storm and ice were to blame."

Joy shook her head. "No. I remember everything. Most of it anyway. But it's still mixed-up. Like watching a movie with lots of interruptions. Some things are out of sequence."

"Tell me. Maybe it'll help to sort it out if you talk through what you remember."

She balled the tissue up in her fist. "I remember leaving the office. I called Chad and told him I was on my way. The snow was so thick I could barely see to drive, but I wanted to get home to Mikey. I remember a red light and I slowed down, then I must have hit some ice because I was suddenly moving forward and spinning and I saw a flash and then nothing."

"What do you remember next?"

"Waking up in the hospital. My head was splitting. There was a policeman there but I don't remember why. There was another one a few days later who talked about a citation." Joy rubbed her temple. "I don't remember anything until Grandma came and told me it was officially an accident and everything was fine, but I didn't know what she was talking about."

"I do." Willa patted Joy's knee. "I spoke with Nell often when you were in the hospital. The police thought the accident was caused because you were distracted. They found your cell phone nearby and assumed you were using it. But then they did an investigation and decided you were not at fault."

"Did they say why?"

Willa shook her head. "Nell never said. She was so relieved it was settled and she had her hands full taking care of you and Mikey after...well, you know."

Joy pressed her lips together and bowed her head. "Even though it was an accident, I'm the one who ran into Simon's car. It's still my fault."

"Don't do this to yourself, sweetheart."

Willa's cell rang and she groaned. "It's probably him again. Are you going to talk to him?"

"I can't. I can't ever face him again."

Willa silenced her phone. "I'm sure he'll forgive you."

Joy shook her head. "No. You don't know how deeply he's hurting, how fierce his anger runs. I love him too much to ask him to forgive. He'll hate me if he learns what I did."

"He loves you, too, sweetie. He might have trouble at first but in time…"

Joy stood. "I can't stay here. I can't be around him knowing. Willa, what am I going to do?"

"Leave it to me. My sister-in-law, Emily, lives in Pass Christian. She has a big house on the beach and she owns a very nice gift shop. You and Mikey will like it there and she'll welcome you with open arms and spoil you rotten. I'm going to pick up Mikey and then I'll make all the arrangements."

Willa hadn't been gone five minutes when someone knocked on the door. Joy peered through the peephole and saw Simon. Her insides caught fire. She rested her head against the door, keeping as silent as possible and praying he'd go away if she didn't answer.

"Willa. Is Joy there? Open up, please. I need to talk to you. Joy?"

He knocked a few more times then left. Joy's knees threatened to give way. Oh, how she needed his strength and support. The very things she was forever denied now. Her only option was to take Willa's advice and leave town. Pass Christian was only two hours away— not nearly far enough, but it would have to do.

Maybe with time and distance she could find a way to stop loving Simon and start her life over.

Again.

Simon rested his hands on his knees, sucking in deep breaths. Running was a waste of time and effort. This was his second five-mile run today and he didn't feel any different. Physically fatigued but emotionally tormented. A hot shower and a bite to eat did nothing, either.

Out on the front porch, he leaned against the post. He couldn't stand being in the office without Joy there. It had been three days since she'd left. He'd pestered Willa to death with no result. He was at his wit's end. One minute he was fighting anger over Joy's fault in the accident and the next he was worried that she was alone and dealing with the guilt. He loved her but he'd loved his wife, too, and she was gone because of Joy. The woman he loved now.

His mind was on a carousel that was gaining speed with no way off. His gaze traveled toward the garden where the Blessing Bridge stood. A need to visit filled his thoughts but he shut it down.

What was he supposed to do about his conflicting emotions? He breathed a sigh of relief when he saw Ray's car coming up the driveway. He could use a diversion and a different opinion. Simon met him as he got out of the car.

"What brings you by?"

"I thought I'd bring good news in person. And I need a favor."

Simon started to stroll down the drive, needing to

move and prevent his mind from dwelling on things for which he had no answers. "I could use good news."

"You've sold the hotel. The buyer agreed to your counteroffer. Sheila said she tried to call you but you didn't answer."

"Yeah, I've had a lot on my mind." They walked along in silence. Simon searched for a way to explain. He stopped and rested his arms on an old fence. "I found out who the driver of the other car was." Ray waited quietly. "Joy."

"What? No, that can't be right."

Simon quickly filled him in on the report, Joy's departure and his struggle to process the news. "Why would she run away?"

Ray sighed. "Maybe because you've made your feelings clear about the driver of the car? You've been very vocal about what you'd like to do to that person. I'm not surprised she left. She was probably terrified of what you might do."

"I would never hurt her. I love her."

"No surprise there. And she loves you. Look at this from her side. How do you think it made her feel? To a woman like Joy, with her compassionate heart, learning that she caused your greatest pain would be devastating. She might never get over it."

Simon's stomach clenched. The thought of Joy enduring that kind of overwhelming guilt wounded him to the core of his being.

Ray shifted to face him. "I think it's time you took a hard look at yourself, my friend, and your attitudes. This anger and resentment you've been nursing has to end. You've lived in this pity party too long."

Simon considered punching his friend in the jaw but the impulse died quickly. He couldn't condemn the man for telling the truth. He pushed away from the fence. "What was the favor you wanted?"

"I have a meeting in Savannah tomorrow. I could use a good pilot and a plane to get me there."

"Sure. Just let me know when you want to leave."

"Thanks. And, Simon… It's time to let go and move on. You deserve to be happy again. I told you Joy would be a blessing. All you have to do is accept it."

Simon fixed a cool drink and went to his office later that evening. He'd gone to the theater meeting tonight. Partly to keep his mind occupied but mostly because he'd come to enjoy being involved. He liked the people and teaching Arlo carpentry, and because it was Joy's happy place.

He'd worried that it might be awkward dodging questions about why Joy wasn't there, but Willa must have put out a rumor that Joy was on vacation. He doubted she was having a good time. His gaze drifted to the alcove and his heart lurched. She should be here. He wanted her here. No, he didn't. She'd taken everything away from him. He pushed up from the chair and paced. He had to find a solution.

Ray had told him to step back and look at the big picture and let go of the past. In his heart Simon knew his friend was right. He couldn't bear the thought of Joy living with the guilt. But how did he forgive her? How could he dismiss it as if it didn't matter? If he forgave her, he'd be telling Joy what she'd done was all right.

A dark cloud descended on his mind, and his breathing came short. His emotions were at odds, tearing him in two like a medieval torture rack. He loved Joy but he'd loved Holly, too. There was no way to reconcile the two sides. One woman had taken the other.

The cloud in his mind grew darker and denser. He fought to control his raging emotions. Anger merged with grief, which in turn mixed with love and confusion. He walked into Joy's office looking for an answer, a direction. His gaze landed on the small flyer for the bicentennial lying on the corner of her desk. In the center was a drawing of the Blessing Bridge.

Maybe the answers were there. Hadn't Duke said something about forgiveness that night at the theater? So had Ray. Visiting the bridge would be a futile gesture but he couldn't remain in this state of divide. A few minutes later he pulled into the parking lot at the bridge. The sign said Closed After Dark, but he owned the place. He could go whenever he wanted.

The closer he drew to the bridge, the harder his heart pounded and the more heightened his emotions became. His spirit grew heavy. He was drowning in the dark alone.

His soul was weary and burdened as he stepped onto the bridge. He grasped the railing knowing what he had to do but afraid. He searched frantically for answers to his torment, but he knew there was nowhere else to turn. It was time to admit he was lost and defeated.

The Lord had finally called him to account. He had to forgive. Everyone. Everything. He had to let go of the blame and the anger. Every molecule in him rebelled, but he knew he had no choice. *Father. Help me.*

Simon bent forward over the rail. He'd vowed to

never forgive what had been done to him, but he was overwhelmed. He couldn't do this alone. Slowly, he lowered himself down to rest his back against the railing, too weak to stand.

He closed his eyes, looking back at how he'd come to be in this position. Nothing in his life was the way he'd believed. Not the town, not the people and now not the accident. From somewhere deep inside, the words formed in his mind, as if someone else was telling him what to say. He forgave his father, the people of Blessing. He forgave Holly for dying. And Joy for driving the car that night. Lastly he asked for forgiveness for himself. His pride, his arrogance and his selfish attitude.

When he finished he felt completely drained but oddly light. He looked up at the sky and saw the full moon shining through the trees like a beacon, reminding him of the source of all light.

For the first time he saw everything clearly and the path he'd taken to get here. His troubled childhood, the resentment toward the town and his grief over the accident all lay before him. With a clear mind, he could see that loving again didn't mean Holly hadn't mattered. Loving Joy and Mikey didn't replace his wife and child—it was only a new direction. The accident was a traffic event caused by an unexpected storm, not some divine punishment.

Holly wouldn't want him to be mired in grief. She'd been a practical woman who believed that life went on and each day was a gift from the Lord that should be enjoyed.

He stood, his thoughts focused on Joy. She'd started awakening him from the day they'd met. She had been his biggest blessing. His gaze lowered to the water in the pond and the reflected image of the moon. His heart opened for the first time in years and inside he found joy. His Joy.

He sent up another prayer, one of thanksgiving. He was free and he had to find Joy.

Despite his best night's sleep in months, Simon woke filled with anxious energy. He had to find Joy. He had to bring her back. By the end of the day, he was on the verge of giving up hope. Willa still ignored his calls. And now, because of his persistence in keeping away from the people of Blessing, he had no one else to turn to. Maybe it was time to accept that things had gone too far between him and Joy to be restored. His stubbornness had cost him the thing he loved most. Joy would never be for him. His heart was hers but she didn't want it.

He lifted his head, his gaze falling on the calendar. The date reminded him that the lease on the bridge land loomed. Suddenly he knew what he could do. He might not be able to have Joy in his life, but he could give her the desire of her heart. The one thing she'd asked him for. The bridge land.

Pulling out his phone, he called Ray. "I need you to take care of something right away."

Joy held Mikey a little closer to her side, kissed the top of his head and kept the old wooden porch swing moving slowly. It was raining and she and her little boy had come out to the front porch to enjoy the weather. The rain hitting the tin roof gave her a measure of comfort.

Willa's sister-in-law, Emily, had been a wonderful

hostess, spoiling her and Mikey to extremes. She'd even hired Joy to work in her shop part-time. The large house was charming and welcoming, and she had plenty of private time. But it wasn't home. Blessing was home.

"I like watching it rain, don't you, Mommy?"

"I do. When I was your age, my mom and I would sit on our porch and watch it rain. Sometimes I'd bring my toys out and other times I'd color in one of my books."

Mikey reached over and tugged his dog closer. "I like having Pickles here." He was silent a long moment, then he looked up at her, his blue eyes troubled. "When can we go home? I miss Willa and my friends at school."

She wasn't sure how to answer him. "It won't be much longer. Aren't you having fun here on the beach and staying with Miss Emily?"

"Yes, ma'am. But why didn't Mr. Simon come, too? He's our best friend, isn't he?"

Joy's heart ached. He was so much more than a friend. "Yes, but he has work to do."

"Will he come and visit us soon?"

If only. Nothing would make her happier. "I'm not sure." She was sure. Willa had told her the hotel had sold. Simon had accomplished his goal. He'd sold his inheritance and now he could leave Blessing and return to his life. Once he was gone, they would go home.

The diner had opened yesterday and she hated that she wasn't there to help. Willa had also confirmed that the bridge land was still in limbo. The deadline was only a day away. The thought made her want to cry. She'd come to understand much about Simon and his attitudes toward Blessing, but she'd never fully grasped his feelings about the bridge.

Emily came out onto the porch carrying a tray. "I brought you some sweet tea and fresh sugar cookies."

"Yummy." Mikey scooted off the swing and picked a cookie from the plate. "I love these."

Emily laughed. "Good thing because I love baking them." She sat in the chair beside the swing and smiled. "How are you doing today?"

"Fine. Enjoying the rain."

"This big old porch was the reason we bought the house. That and the fact that it was across from the beach. After Hurricane Katrina, I wasn't sure we could rebuild, but the Lord made a way."

Joy doubted he'd make a way for her this time. Emily must have sensed her mood.

"Don't give up hope, honey. Even when it looks like there's no solution, no possible way, things can sort themselves out. Remember, the Lord is in control and He knows what you need and when you need it. Timing is in His hands."

Joy tried to cling to that thought the rest of the day. Working at the gift shop gave her a purpose and kept her mind and her heart from yearning for Simon. She was finishing her shift when her cell phone rang. Willa. It wasn't like her to call during the day, especially now that the diner was open again. Her concern rose as she answered. "Hey, Willa. Is everything all right?" Joy was surprised to hear her cousin chuckle.

"Oh yes, things are very all right. I'm sending you a picture that's going to make your day. Hang on."

Joy waited a moment then checked her text messages. The image was from the headline on the front page of the *Blessing Banner*. "Baker Donates Blessing

Bridge." Stunned, Joy could only stare in amazement. "When did this happen?"

"Yesterday. Big shock, huh? Would you believe Simon marched right into the mayor's office and handed him all the paperwork? Not only that but he also donated enough money for the property to be landscaped and—"

"There's more?"

"Oh yes. He included the old mansion and gave the city permission to decide how best to utilize it for the future."

"I don't know what to say." Her mind was spinning. Why had Simon suddenly changed his mind? What had happened since she'd been gone? She wanted to talk to him but that wasn't possible.

She had to set thoughts of Simon aside and be grateful that the bridge was safe at last. She might never know what had persuaded him to donate the land, but she would be forever grateful. And her love for him only grew stronger.

Simon looked up as Ray entered his office, a strange expression on his face. His first thought was something had happened to Joy.

Ray anticipated his question and shook his head. "Nothing's wrong. In fact, I have some interesting news for you about the accident."

Simon rubbed his forehead. "There's nothing you can say that will change anything."

"Oh yes, there is. Take a look at this." He handed Simon a paper.

"It's the accident report. I've seen it."

"Look closer." Ray took a seat.

Simon picked up the paper. "Can't you just tell me?"

"All right. This is the report after the investigation. Initially the police assumed Joy had been driving distracted and had failed to stop for the intersection. But that's not what happened. There was a third car. A teenager, newly licensed and inexperienced driving in snow, especially the kind that was blowing that night. He failed to stop soon enough, rammed into the back of Joy's car and sent her careening into the intersection." He leaned forward with a smile. "It wasn't her fault, Simon. It was no one's fault, really. A result of the weather."

Simon went over what his friend had said. Was it possible? Was Joy a victim as much as Holly had been? Realization clawed up through his system. He scraped his fingers over his scalp. "What have I done? I chased her away because I thought—"

"You didn't have the whole story. Neither did Joy."

He'd already come to terms with her part in the accident. Now he found that it wasn't what either of them had thought. His relief quickly dissolved into shame and regret. How had he gotten everything so wrong? His emotions were roiling like an angry sea.

Pride. He'd clung to his stubborn pride instead of allowing his grief to heal and his heart to love again. A swell of determination supplanted his emotions. "I have to find her. I have to let her know what really happened. I can't let her go on thinking she's caused me pain when it wasn't her fault." He'd sought and given forgiveness, but now he needed to seek hers.

"I agree. How do you propose to do that?"

"I don't know. I've run out of options."

Ray stood. "You know, Willa's Diner reopened. She's there all the time now. She has Joy's best interests at heart. She wouldn't want her to suffer needlessly."

A short while later, Simon stood across the street from Willa's Diner trying to find the courage to cross the street. He was going to make one last attempt to find Joy. He'd beg in front of the whole diner if he had to. If that failed, then he'd have to accept he'd lost Joy forever and return to Charlotte. The idea held no appeal at all. Blessing was home now, but he couldn't stay here without Joy and Mikey.

Willa looked stunned when he entered. The patrons all started to clap and cheer, thanking him for saving the bridge. She hurried toward him, took his arm and led him to a booth in a quiet corner.

"What are you doing here?"

"I need to talk to her, Willa. Please."

She frowned and set her hands on her hips. "Well, she doesn't want to talk to you."

"Please, listen. Ray brought me a second report on the accident. It wasn't Joy's fault. It really was an accident."

"So you needed proof to set aside your anger? You couldn't just forgive and move on? I'm not sure she'll want to hear that."

"No. This isn't about me. I love her, Willa. I can't let her go on thinking she's done something horrible to me. I don't want her carrying a burden of guilt she doesn't deserve. Please, Willa. Joy and Mikey mean everything to me. I want her to know the truth and that I love them. If she wants nothing to do with me, then..."

He swallowed. The very thought turned his blood cold. "I'll leave and never bother her again."

Willa held his gaze a long moment. "Do you like the beach?"

"What?"

"The Pass is really nice this time of year."

Simon was tempted to shake the information out of the woman. "What Pass?"

"Pass Christian. It's a small town on the Mississippi coast. My sister-in-law, Emily, lives there. She has a house on the beach. A large house with plenty of room for company."

"Is that where she is? How do I find her?"

Willa shrugged. "Can't say. I promised I wouldn't tell you where she was, and I keep my promises."

"Do you have an address or a phone number?" His hopes were rising but he feared Willa would force him to search every house on the coast to atone for his sins.

"I'd have to look it up and I'm busy. Emily doesn't like people calling and dropping by Morning Glory Cottage willy-nilly."

Simon grabbed her and planted a kiss on her cheek. "I'll love you forever." Spinning on his heel, he went to his truck, climbed in and turned the wheel toward the Gulf Coast. Two hours later he was driving along Highway 90 praying that his journey wouldn't be in vain. He barely glanced at the Gulf waters lapping onto the beach on his left. His gaze was trained on the passing signs. His heart leaped when he saw the Welcome to Pass Christian sign. He hoped his GPS could find Morning Glory Cottage without an address.

"In one quarter mile you will reach your destination."

Simon slowed, looking for a sign or something to identify the cottage.

"You destination is on the right."

The sign hanging on the picket fence displayed the name of the charming beach home. Morning Glory Cottage was right out of a painting. He pulled into the narrow drive and stopped, wondering if this was such a good idea after all. Now that he was here, he had some explaining to do and he wasn't sure he could accomplish that well enough to make Joy believe him.

He lowered his head. No. This wasn't about him. He was here to free Joy from guilt she didn't deserve. Nothing more. Climbing out of the car, he then approached the front door, hands clammy and shaking. His knock was quickly answered by a woman in her sixties with white hair and a cheery smile. She didn't give him a chance to explain.

"You must be Joy's Simon. I've been expecting you."

Caught off guard, Simon searched for a reply. "I, uh, yes. I'm Simon. Is she here?"

The woman frowned. "I'm sorry. You just missed her."

Simon's hopes plummeted. "Do you know when she'll be back?"

"No, but I think you can still catch her. Just cross the road to the beach and go that way."

There was a mischievous twinkle in the woman's eyes that sent his hopes soaring again.

"And, young man, be sweet when you find her. She's very fragile right now. She's nursing a broken heart. I hope you can help her with that."

Simon jogged across the street and onto the beach.

He peered in the direction the woman had indicated but didn't see anyone. Picking up his pace, he trudged through the sand, searching the landscape for a woman with auburn hair.

He saw her then. She'd been sitting on the sea wall and had started to walk again. She wore a blue dress that floated around her calves and flattered her trim figure. The sun brought out the burnished strands of her hair. His heart swelled with love. He started to jog.

"Joy!"

She stopped and turned around. He quickened his steps. When he drew close, she wrapped her arms around her waist and turned her back. A lance of fear coursed through him. Was he too late? Would she even give him a chance to explain, to tell her how much he loved her?

"Go away, Simon. Please."

He started to reach out for her but her posture clearly warned him to keep his distance. "Joy, please hear me out. It's important." She shook her head. His hopes began to crumble. He had no idea how he'd go on if she shut him out. He couldn't let her go on thinking she'd been guilty of something that wasn't her fault. He took a deep breath and stepped off his emotional cliff.

"Joy. I love you."

Simon's presence was wreaking havoc on her senses. She felt his warmth and strength and breathed in the scent of his aftershave. His confession of love sucked all her feelings into a whirlpool of pain and hope. Her heart pounded erratically, her palms grew clammy, and her hopes rose and fell on giant swells of emotion. She tried to regain her composure but couldn't. She'd imagined him coming for her a thousand times. Watching him stride toward her across the sand matched every fantasy she'd envisioned. He was more handsome than she'd remembered. Now he was here and she had no idea how to act or what to say.

She swallowed and faced him. "What are you doing here? I thought you'd be back in Charlotte by now."

"Why would I be there when you're here?"

She tried to ignore the leap of hope his words created. "Because you sold the hotel and now you're free from your inheritance."

"But not free from you."

She risked a glance at his eyes. "Simon, please. Just go. Say what you have to and leave. Please."

"I said it. I love you."

The tenderness in his voice nearly weakened her resolve. "You can't. Not after knowing that I…"

"No, you don't understand. Please look at this." He handed her a folded piece of paper.

"What is it?"

"Read it, please."

She took it, glancing at the top of the page, her heart aching anew. "It's the accident report. I've seen it."

"No, this is the second one. After the investigation." He stepped around her, searching her face.

"What investigation?"

Simon rubbed his forehead. "The one they did after the storm passed. They did more detailed investigations of all of the serious accidents. That's not important now. The point is, the crash wasn't your fault. You were hit from behind and sent into the intersection. It wasn't your fault."

She had no idea what he was talking about. She'd never heard about a follow-up inquiry into the crash. Joy took a closer look at the document, focusing on the notes on the incident. A huge weight lifted from her spirit. She hadn't been careless or distracted or lost control of her car. She'd been hit from behind. She wasn't to blame. She touched her forehead, feeling light-headed.

Closing her eyes, she whispered a heartfelt prayer of thanksgiving. At least she could move forward now without the crushing guilt. "That's good. I'm relieved that I didn't… That I wasn't…" She handed back the paper. "It doesn't change anything."

He reached out and grasped her shoulders. "But it does."

"No. It was still my car that hit yours, and every time you look at me you'll remember and I'll remember and it'll eventually destroy us."

"Joy, I came here to tell you that I've let go."

"Let go?"

"Of the anger and resentment, the pride that's been keeping me locked in the past in grief and anger. The Lord and I had a serious talk. He reminded me that forgiveness isn't for the other person. It's for me. To free me to be closer to Him. He showed me that I couldn't move forward until I forgave the past. It's the hardest thing I've ever had to do. I even forgave my father."

Joy struggled to absorb what Simon was telling her. "I'm glad, Simon. I know you'll be happy again someday." She started to touch him then pulled back. She needed to walk away before she lost her courage. She stepped around him then halted. "Thank you for saving the bridge."

He took her arm in his hand. "Thank you for saving me."

"What?" His grip was firm yet gentle and it was all she could do to keep from leaning into him.

"You rescued me, Joy. You brought me back to life and gave me hope. You reminded me what living was about and you dragged me from that cave I'd been hiding in."

She met his gaze, letting her happiness for him override her heartache. He may have forgiven everyone, but there was little hope for them, despite his profession of love. She raised her hand and placed her palm over his scarred cheek. "I'm glad you've found peace finally, Simon. You deserve to be happy." He laid his hand over hers, and she lost herself in his touch.

"I love you, Joy. And I love Mikey and I want us to be a family."

She searched his gaze. He couldn't be serious. "You'll be leaving. You have your business to start."

He took her shoulders in his hands. "No. I'm not going back. I have a new plan. I'm going to start my air service right here only on a smaller scale. Besides, I have to teach Arlo to fly, remember? I already bought his manual."

Joy grabbed the opportunity to divert the subject. "How are things going with Arlo?"

"Fine. He got community service like Ray expected. He's going to be fine. I gave him his first flight lesson. He's a natural. Joy, I don't want to talk about Arlo."

He turned her toward him, his gaze caressing her face. "I'm going to stay in Blessing."

She tried to pull away. "I heard you got an offer on the estate. That's the last piece of your inheritance. You're free at last."

"I turned it down." He brushed a strand of wind-blown hair from her cheek. "I'm going to keep the estate and the old house. I think it needs to be made livable again."

"Good. It deserves to be restored."

"It does, and I want you and Mikey to stay with me. I love you. I want you to marry me and spend the rest of your life with me."

The tenderness in his voice was her undoing. Tears formed behind her eyes. "I love you, too, Simon. But I didn't think…"

He pulled her into his arms. "We've done enough thinking. Will you marry me and let me be part of your family?"

She smiled, her heart threatening to burst from her chest. "Yes. Oh yes."

Simon pulled her into his arms and kissed her with all the promise of the future. Her heart overflowed with love and the sense of belonging wrapped around her like a soft cloud. Her hermit had emerged from his cave and transformed into a warm and loving man who would cherish her and Mikey forever.

Through all the heartache, loss and grief, the Lord had made a way.

"Mr. Simon!"

They turned to see Mikey racing toward them across the beach, Pickles leading the way. Emily waved from behind him. Her son tripped and fell in the sand then got up and continued to run. The happiness on his face brought tears to Joy's eyes. He raised his arms as he drew near Simon, who grabbed him up in a big hug.

"I missed you so much."

"I missed you too, little buddy."

Mikey placed his small hands on Simon's cheeks and Joy couldn't help but smile. One little damaged hand, one damaged face and two damaged hearts all made whole again with forgiveness and love.

"I saw you kissing my mommy. Does this mean you're going to be my daddy?"

Simon met her gaze, the light in his eyes brighter than she'd ever seen.

"Would you like that?"

Mikey's answer was a choke hold around Simon's neck. Simon shifted the tiny body in his arms and wrapped his free arm around Joy's waist. "Then let's go home."

Together, Simon, Mikey, Joy and Pickles walked across the beach, finally a family.

* * * * *

*If you loved this tale of sweet romance,
pick up these other books
from author Lorraine Beatty.*

Her Fresh-Start Family
Their Family Legacy
Their Family Blessing
The Orphans' Blessing
Her Secret Hope

Available now from Love Inspired!

Find more great reads at www.LoveInspired.com

Dear Reader,

I hope you enjoyed the next visit to Blessing, Mississippi, and getting to know Simon and Joy. Their journey was difficult in many ways, each battling loss, broken dreams and big changes in their lives. For Simon, the biggest challenge was coming to see that his past wasn't exactly like he remembered. In fact, nothing was the way he thought it was.

I think we've all had those moments when we look back and realize that there was more going on in our families and our situations than we understood at the time. Often we have to take a step back and reassess what we thought was real and true. As children we aren't always fully aware of all that goes on in our world, nor do we have the maturity to look at things with full understanding.

That's why it's important not to hold grudges or level blame until we can see the whole picture and collect all the facts. Sometimes that means we have to let go of what we think we know and be willing to look at things honestly. And then forgive.

Love and forgiveness were the only answer to Simon and Joy's situation. Then they could have their happy ending.

I love hearing from readers. You can contact me through my website at lorrainebeatty.com, my Facebook page, Lorraine Beatty Author, and @lorrainebeatty on Twitter.

Lorraine

WE HOPE YOU ENJOYED
THIS BOOK FROM

LOVE INSPIRED
INSPIRATIONAL ROMANCE

Uplifting stories of faith, forgiveness and hope.

Fall in love with stories where faith helps
guide you through life's challenges, and discover
the promise of a new beginning.

6 NEW BOOKS AVAILABLE EVERY MONTH!

HARLEQUIN

*Uplifting or passionate,
heartfelt or thrilling—
Harlequin has your
happily-ever-after.*

With a wide range of romance series that each
offer new books every month, you are sure to
find the satisfying escape you deserve.

**Look for all Harlequin series
new releases on the
last Tuesday of each month
in stores and online!**

Harlequin.com

HONSALE0521

COMING NEXT MONTH FROM
Love Inspired

AN AMISH BABY FOR CHRISTMAS
Indiana Amish Brides • by Vannetta Chapman
In danger of losing her farm after her husband's death, pregnant widow Abigail Yutzy needs help—even if she can't afford it. And the local bishop is sure Amish property manager Thomas Albrecht is the perfect person to lend a hand. But can their uneasy holiday alliance heal both their hearts?

THE AMISH OUTCAST'S HOLIDAY RETURN
by Lacy Williams
Grace Beiler knows the Amish faith demands forgiveness, but she still can't understand why her father would offer a job and a place to stay to Zach Miller—the man whose teenage mistake cost her sister's fiancé his life. But as she gets to know him, even family loyalty might not be able to keep her from falling for Zach...

THE PRODIGAL'S HOLIDAY HOPE
Wyoming Ranchers • by Jill Kemerer
Hired to work on his childhood ranch at Christmas, Sawyer Roth's determined to prove he's a changed man. The new owner's daughter, Tess Malone, will be the hardest to convince. But as the single mom and her toddler son wriggle into his heart, can he put the past behind him and start over?

THE PATH NOT TAKEN
Kendrick Creek • by Ruth Logan Herne
After her ex left her pregnant and alone, Devlyn McCabe never planned to tell him about their little boy—but now Rye Bauer's back. Returning to Kendrick Creek temporarily for his job, Rye knew he'd see Devlyn again, but he's shocked to discover he's a father. Can the truth give them a second chance at forever?

SNOWED IN FOR CHRISTMAS
by Gabrielle Meyer
For travel journalist Zane Harris, his little girls are his top priority. So when a holiday snowstorm strands them with the secret mother of his eldest daughter, he's not sure he can allow Liv Butler to bond with the child she gave up as a teen. But Liv might just be exactly what his family needs...

CLAIMING HIS CHRISTMAS INHERITANCE
by C.J. Carroll
In her last matchmaking attempt, Zed Evans's late aunt insisted he get married and live in the family home with his bride for three months if he wants to claim his inheritance. So he proposes to a virtual stranger. But three holidays as Tasha Jenkins's husband could have this confirmed bachelor wishing for a lifetime...

LOOK FOR THESE AND OTHER LOVE INSPIRED BOOKS WHEREVER BOOKS ARE SOLD, INCLUDING MOST BOOKSTORES, SUPERMARKETS, DISCOUNT STORES AND DRUGSTORES.

LICNM1021